A VOICE
FROM THE LIVING

A VOICE
FROM THE LIVING

MARC LOVELL

PUBLISHED FOR THE CRIME CLUB BY

DOUBLEDAY & COMPANY, INC.

GARDEN CITY, NEW YORK

1978

All of the characters in this book
are fictitious, and any resemblance
to actual persons, living or dead,
is purely coincidental.

ISBN: 0-385-14104-1
Library of Congress Catalog Card Number 77-92221
Copyright © 1978 by Doubleday & Company, Inc.
All Rights Reserved
Printed in the United States of America
First Edition

A VOICE
FROM THE LIVING

ONE

The Rolls-Royce stood grandly among middle-income rabble. The parking metre said that the car was safe for another half hour. There were few people about here, though thirty feet away the crowds were passing thickly along Oxford Street.

Jill Parr glanced both ways and across the road. No one was watching. She stepped to the passenger door of the Rolls-Royce, took hold of the handle, pressed its button with her thumb. The button sank.

The car was unlocked.

Jill's heart had been tripping at a faster pace than normal for the past two minutes, ever since she had stopped near the limousine. Now, her pulsebeat quickened still further. It felt like forefingers of admonition tapping on various parts of her body.

She was afraid, stunned, amazed. But she didn't release the handle and step back. She looked around again and saw again that all was clear.

So go on, she thought. Do it.

Jill Parr drew the door open. Nothing happened—no bells rang, no angry voice shouted, no footsteps came up in a rush. Leaving the door standing wide, she got in.

The leather gave beneath Jill welcomingly. After savouring that for some seconds, she shifted sideways and moved to the other seat. She clasped the steering wheel, pressed her shoulders into the seat back, tapped her toe on the accelerator, gazed ahead beyond the flying lady mascot. Her heart was racing.

That's it, she thought. No more.

She slid quickly over to the other side, got out, slammed the door and moved away. While still telling herself that running would be a mistake, she started to run.

Jill reached the Oxford Street crowds. There she was forced to slow. She hated it. She wanted to be either moving at full speed or hidden from view. Preferably the latter. She couldn't stand the idea of being looked at. She felt partly undressed.

The entrance to a department store appeared on her right. Jill went through it, pushing past dawdlers. Inside, there was no hope of speed, but there would be washrooms. She could hide herself in a stall.

About to move to the rear, Jill saw a closer answer. It was a self-service photo kiosk. She went to it swiftly, sat on the stool and shot the curtain across.

Jill sagged. She stared dully at the floor. Until her pulses steadied and her fear drained, she thought of nothing. She was left with the amazement. It caused her to shake her head long and slowly.

Jill took cigarettes and lighter from her purse, lit up and drew with greed at the smoke. What, she thought calmly, is wrong with me today? Why did I get that sudden urge to sit in the Rolls? It was crazy. If I'd been caught, naturally they would've assumed I was trying to steal the car. Crazy.

Suddenly Jill giggled. She being hidden here and safe, the adventure had lost much of its weirdness, all its danger. She reminded herself that she had never sat at the wheel of a Rolls-Royce in her life and that today was her birthday. So there. She had been treating herself to something really quite harmless. A fun escapade.

There came the niggling thought that she, Jill Parr, private secretary to the head of Almanacum Imports Ltd., a position of consequence, was not the type for escapades of any nature.

"Okay then," she said, lifting her chin, but still smiling. "It's my age." Like many people who live alone, Jill had the habit of talking to herself.

"They say you change every seven years. This is it. I'm twenty-eight. From now on I'll probably turn into one of those extroverts who do wild and wonderful things and wear kinky clothes all the time. Great."

Jill dropped her cigarette and ground it out underfoot. Leaving the photo booth, she went to the nearest counter to look at scarves. She retained a faint smile. Jill was, in a way, proud of herself for having done the outrageous. She only regretted that she had no confidante with whom she could share it.

Which, as she turned a scarf over in her hands, led to a thought that took away the lingering smile. It was a bit sad that she had to be buying her own birthday present. Though true enough the typing pool had clubbed together to get her a writing case, and big boss Mr. Olivieri had given her a book token.

Trouble was, of course, she had no current boy friend. She had been off the male for weeks, since discovering on the second date with John that he was married. She wasn't having any of that sleazy nonsense. Before that, Frank had been given the push finally because he was only after one thing. Before Frank, months ago, it had been herself who had been dropped, though gently, by Ben Armitage. Too bad about that. Ben was a charmer, kind and with beautiful manners.

Jill sighed. Then she came out of her reverie with a start on being addressed by a salesgirl. Lifting her chin—another habit —Jill said, "Just browsing, thank you."

She moved on. She left the store and ambled through the heavy, Saturday crowd. To put a cap on her previous thoughts, end them neatly, she told herself that career girls had to accept a bit of loneliness as part of their chosen way.

Some minutes later, while waiting to be served in a busy candy shop, Jill had the sensation that she was being watched. It was there in a chillness up her spine and across her shoulders, a feeling of warmth in the nape of her neck. Oddly, it made her tighten her forehead.

Not displeased, Jill looked slowly and casually around. She expected to meet the gaze of some man, catch him in the act of appraisal. She would freeze him with a haughty glare. At least, she hoped she would. Perhaps today . . .

But she saw no man looking at her, no person at all looking at her, even though she turned in a full circle. Back facing the counter, she found the sensation had gone. Some passing Romeo, she mused, unconcerned.

After buying a box of her favourite chocolates, Jill went outside. She strolled, enjoying the outing and the company of the other shoppers.

Like most women on this summer day, Jill wore a cotton dress. Hers was of simple cut and a plain blue. The belt accentuated her shapely figure, the colour brought out the blue of her eyes. She was medium height and weight. Her complexion, like dogma, appeared flawless. She was clever with cosmetics. Her short brown hair with its centre parting was rigidly neat.

Knowing she looked younger than her age, plus having no desperation at the approach of that dread thirty, Jill Parr used none of the tricks to create an illusion of youth: those quick turns to make the hair swing, the face downtilted so that the eyes could perform that dewy upward look, the tiny smiles that pulled no creases, the ingenue's blank stare. Jill had a refreshing naturalness. Being pretty helped.

Over the next fifteen minutes, Jill bought a packet of cigarettes, grinned at a windowful of kittens, and decided to put off buying her birthday present until she could think of something she really wanted.

She came to a life-size dog made of plaster. On its back was a box for donations to the RSPCA. Jill stopped automatically and opened her purse, delving for a small coin. She found one, reached it toward the slot, then paused.

She had an impulse to put the coin back and replace it with something of greater value. Not a larger piece of silver either, but a pound note. Jill blinked. A pound? she thought. Surely that was going too far. No one gave casual donations like that. It was a silly notion.

Yet the impulse grew stronger. It was the same as when she had come to a stop near the Rolls-Royce, had that power. There was a sense of conviction that not to follow the impulse would be wrong.

"Oh, hell," Jill muttered, putting the coin away. She drew a pound note from her billfold, crumpled it up and rammed it into the slot. Guiltily she glanced around. She would have hated to have been seen, and thought a goody-goody.

Farewell to alms, Jill fumed lightly as she went on. If that's not the stupidest thing I've ever done. A whole damn pound. This freaky new me better watch her step or she's going to be in the poorhouse.

However, Jill soon smiled and forgave herself the quixotic act. It was, after all, her birthday.

She went into a large confectioner's, climbed three flights of stairs and entered the cafeteria. Pushing a tray along the rails she chose a beetroot salad, roll and butter, a slice of apple pie and a cup of tea. Paying, she carried her tray in search of a vacant table.

All were occupied. But there were several with empty chairs and sharing was part of the cafeteria philosophy. Jill liked that, and always used it to explain her pleasure whenever she saw no table vacant.

She chose one at which a man sat alone. He was old, white of hair and beard, cheerful of face. He ate while reading the book he had propped against the cruet.

Jill asked, "Do you mind . . . ?"

The old man looked up, smiled and waved a hand of invitation. "I don't own it, love. Make yourself at home."

Jill sat. Within two minutes she and the old man were chatting like old friends with new interests. He told of his boredom in retirement, Jill told of her job, of the flat she'd had since coming to London seven years ago, of her parents up in North Wales. She was obliged to caution herself twice about being a monologuist. She knew that, though sphinxlike in the office, when socialising she tended to overtalk.

After her table companion had finished his meal, had closed his book and left, Jill sat on, eating slowly to pass the time. She ignored the thought that weekends were a bother. She told herself that later she might call one of her few London friends still unmarried. They could go to the movies. She also thought that cafeterias were sad places, and then scoffed at herself.

Plates empty, Jill used up more time by reading a day-old newspaper she found on a nearby chair. It was a girly-murder-scandal tabloid, and she was pleased to find most of its contents offensive. No one came to share the table.

It was when Jill was getting ready to leave that the new urge made itself known.

Its strength and feeling of rightness were the same as the others. It touched not on the emotions. It was a cogitation, a rational statement of what should be done.

The urge was telling Jill that she should go to the counter and complain that her tea had been cold.

Slowly, she settled down on her chair in a slump. She was appalled. Her tea hadn't been piping hot, true, but neither had it been lukewarm, let alone cold. That was the kind of complaint made by fussy nuisances. She wasn't like that. The reverse. She hated scenes. In restaurants particularly. She had always been vaguely in awe of waiters, though she didn't know why. There would have to be some great wrong in a cafe before she would complain.

So this was out of the question. She was being plain stupid. Was she merely trying to turn her birthday shopping trip into a big event?

"Ridiculous," Jill mumbled. She got up, collected her purse and her box of chocolates, moved away from the table. She set off toward the glass swing doors. Midway there, she turned and headed for the counter.

Her mouth sagged open. She told herself that she was not really doing this, or that she was going to buy something else to eat, a cake, or that she was going to ask for some kind of information. Her emotions quavered.

Jill passed the end of the queue of people waiting with trays. She edged between them and the rail. She was unaware of being given hostile looks by those who took her for a line-jumper. Her eyes were fixed on the girl who stood serving at the drinks section.

Jill felt strange, wretched. She felt like a pupil on her way to the principal's office for punishment. There was gooseflesh on her bare arms. Elsewhere, she was sweaty. She was both determined to go through with her decision and acutely embarrassed.

She stopped opposite the girl, who looked at her and chanted, "Milk, tea or coffee?"

Jill heard herself say, "I've had my lunch. And I want you to know that my tea was cold. Stone cold. It's a disgrace. I ought to report you to the manager."

The girl gaped. Jill's embarrassment won. In any case, the mission over, the urge had gone. Flushing brightly, trying and failing to smile, or to say the blow-softening words she wanted to say, Jill turned and hurried back along the line of people. Her mind was dull with shock.

Not slowing beyond the glass doors, she went to the stairs and clattered down. On one landing she dropped her box of chocolates but let it lie there. While hustling along the next landing she had the feeling that she was being followed, but didn't look back or stand still to find out.

On the ground floor she pushed through a group of shoppers and went along the aisle almost at a run. That, she knew, was the worst thing you could do in a store, they would think you were a thief, but she couldn't help herself. She wanted to be away from the place.

She passed through an exit. At a stride she threaded shoppers as she retraced her steps. No longer did she have the feeling of being followed. She turned into the side street and looked away from the Rolls-Royce as she went by.

Two blocks along, Jill came to her Hillman. She felt a gush of love for the familiar possession, adoring its cracked green paintwork and the patches on the convertible top. She hurried to get inside.

Letting herself slide down, Jill lay her head back on the seat. She closed her eyes. Her body was still sweaty where covered. She began to picture the face of the girl behind the counter, but quickly stopped herself.

Sitting up she lit a cigarette. She thought that maybe she had made the complaint because it was something she had always wanted to do; or it was her freaky new *persona;* or perhaps the tea really had been cold and her complaint was justified, but her shyness, her hatred of scenes, had tried to deny that; or . . .

"Oh, what does it matter," Jill said bitterly. "I'm just a bit screwy today, that's all. Let's go home."

Fifteen minutes later Jill was parking in Cheever Street, a quiet road to the north of Regent's Park. The houses were of various designs and sizes but shared the same age, pre-World War One. The house Jill stopped in front of was tall and thin and flat-faced. Although the same rusty brick all over, the trim on its three levels was of different colours, as were the drapes: the original one-family unit had been made into three flats.

As Jill went through the gateway into the tiny patch of front garden, she saw the bottom tenant in her window. They exchanged waves.

Mrs. Parkinson was middle-aged, had a beak face, always wore a scarf tied peasant style over her hair, and was invariably charming to Jill despite having a sour expression.

Two of the three daily bottles of milk were on the step. Jill took hers, leaving the last for the top tenant, Miss Kelly, let herself in and went up one flight of stairs. It was with relief that she arrived in her flat.

It was untidy and comfortable, with a vast living room and one undersized bedroom. Kitchen and bath were adequate. The rental of the flat took exactly half of Jill's pay packet, but she didn't begrudge it. This was home.

She kicked off her pumps as she wandered around the main room with its two saggy couches, easy chairs, bookshelves crammed to the limits with paperbacks, travel posters, and an old, scarred upright piano that she had bought from a pub that was being demolished.

Jill stopped by the window. It showed a view of long gardens and the backs of other houses. There were plenty of trees and flowers. Jill breathed deeply; content.

Swinging around she clapped her hands and said, "Tea." As she walked toward the kitchen she said, "No, coffee." But apart from that, she refused to think about the cafeteria debacle.

Half an hour later, after a shower, Jill was sitting on a couch in her robe, a book in one hand, a cigarette in the other.

She realised she had read halfway down a page without registering a word. Her mind was confused.

Next, the confusion lifted and a concrete thought came through. Jill tensed. Physically, she had already felt like this three times today. She thought of that in order to try to ignore the thought. She also tossed the book aside and stubbed out her cigarette.

The thought persisted. It said, *Go and get Miss Kelly's milk.*

Jill sat quite still. She made no attempt to smile at the fatuousness of her urge. She didn't use logic, argue that she had no use for the milk. She didn't try to understand why she would not only want to steal, but to do so from a kindly neighbour. Jill simply sat there and let the thought run. Which it did, repeatedly.

Go down and take in the bottle of milk.

There was no let up. In one phrasing or another, the thought was revived at intervals of several seconds. It was almost an order. But Jill made no move to obey.

Her one other thought was, I've been neurotic enough for one day, without this.

That didn't help. She was worried.

The thought ended. Jill got up and went over to the telephone, lifted its receiver and dialled one of the numbers that were scrawled on the wall. The call signal was answered with, "May Wilson. Hello."

"Hi, May," Jill said. She was relieved at how normal her voice sounded. "Listen. What're you doing tonight? Oh, too bad. Only there's this super film at the Odeon. You did? Maybe I wouldn't care for it either. Who was your date?"

Nodding, Jill listened as her friend talked about her latest boy friend. She became involved, intrigued. May was the kind who fell in love once a month and whose romances always ended in disaster.

"A dream," May Wilson said. "Talk about handsome."

The conversation moved to other topics. Jill leaned cozily against the wall. She was relaxed and cheerful—until May asked what she had bought for her birthday.

Jill said, "A bottle of milk."

She lifted a hand to cover her mouth, at the same time standing upright. Her tension was back.

May Wilson asked, "What was that?"

Jill said a mechanical, "Excuse me. I have to go. I'll call again later." She put the receiver back in its cradle.

Moving stiffly, she left the room and let herself out of the flat. She went downstairs. She was glad her slippers made no sound. Softly unlatching the front door she drew it open six inches. Squatting, she reached outside and got the milk bottle.

Door closed again, Jill hurried back upstairs and into her flat. She stood in the centre of the room and held the bottle with both hands to her chest. She was trembling.

She stood like that for five minutes, thinking nothing, seeing nothing. It was the former that aroused her finally. The urge. It had gone.

Of course it has, she thought. The act's been done.

Jill felt normal and foolish and still worried. Her trembling had stopped. She looked down at the bottle, turned, went out to the landing and up the top flight of stairs. She put the milk outside Miss Kelly's door.

At which point she thought, a smile growing fast: That's it. Naturally. I didn't want to steal the stupid milk, just bring it in and save the poor old girl a trip downstairs. What a fool I am.

Shaking her head, still smiling, Jill tripped lightly back down to her flat. The smile had a harshness.

Ben Armitage, at thirty-five, had a smooth face and blond curly hair and a suntan. He looked more like a professional golfer than a man who worked in a bank. In height he was average, in build he tended to plumpness—though this was hidden by his Saville Row masterpieces.

Ben had regular features. It was a form of balance that passes for good looks. His mouth was firm, his nose straight, his eyes were grey and steady and attractive. His face had little animation. It told nothing whatever about his personality.

On Monday morning, Ben Armitage was driving his Jaguar into the City. It was well after nine o'clock and the roads had eased from their earlier panic. Ben's position at the bank allowed him a certain amount of tardiness.

He hummed as he drove. He was fairly happy. There was only one thing his life lacked, Ben was musing, and that would come with time. Not too long a time either. Meanwhile—fingers playing over the walnut dashboard—there were toys to give pleasure: the car, extravagant hi-fi, clothes, the speedboat, the high-rise apartment in Highgate Village.

Ben smiled, showing teeth that were white and even but not quite large enough. His flat was a particular entertainment. From the balcony he had a panoramic view of London. That always made him feel good. Also, he was able to amuse his banking acquaintances by pointing out below in Highgate cemetery the headstone of Karl Marx, with the comment, "You could spit on it from here."

He had said that dozens of times and it always got a laugh. It was gratifying for Ben. He was not a man to whom humour came easily. The crack had been made first by someone else.

That someone else Ben thought of now. He thought of Harry Farnsworth at least once a day when away from the bank. It was not obsessional. The image of his superior in Domestic Loans slid quietly in and out of his mind like a cloud passing a window.

The present thought gone, Ben gave his full attention to driving. Traffic was congested now that he had reached the narrow streets of the City, London's financial district. He told himself for the hundredth time that a Mini would be more useful here than a long slinky Jag.

In a lane off Threadneedle Street, Ben turned into an underground garage. One minute later he was back up at street level, walking toward a Victorian building that bore on a brass plate the discreet information, Waringford and Myer, Merchant Bankers.

By the archway entrance, at the foot of steps that on weekdays were carpeted every morning and uncarpeted every night, stood a commissionaire. He was resplendent in grey trousers and weskit, bottle-green frock coat and top hat. The portly man, stiffening at sight of Ben, raised a forefinger salute to his hatbrim.

"Good morning to you, Mr. Armitage."

"And a good morning to you, Mr. Jeb."

It was a comforting little ritual. Ben allowed his smile to last until he had topped the steps and entered a revolving door. When he emerged from that, his face was suitably solemn.

The interior was like a baronial hall. It rose two stories high. A curving staircase climbed to a circling gallery. Below, counters and desks had ample space in which to spread themselves. There was a steady, echoing sound of typewriters and murmuring voices.

Ben's shoes clapped approval as he strode across marble to the stairs. He went up, softly, on more of the red carpeting. Another strip of it ran around the gallery. Up here, silence was needed by the greater minds.

Every door of heavy wood passed by Ben had a name, in gilt. The last one before he turned an elbow was called Harold Farnsworth, Esq. The next door to that said Mr. B. Armitage. You got a first name and the Esq. when you had climbed the last departmental rung.

Ben went into his office. It was small but well furnished, serious but kindly. Colourful drapes softened the venetians, and there were fresh flowers on top of a filing cabinet.

Ben sat at his desk. After a glance all around, which somehow always seemed necessary, he settled to paperwork.

The morning passed. Once Ben buzzed for the secretary he shared with five other executives in Domestic Loans, giving her letters to type from his longhand roughs. Once one of those five looked in to ask if he were free for lunch. Ben said he was not. The man nodded, retreated. He was older than Ben by a good ten years, as were the other four, and all were below Ben on the ladder.

Ben Armitage was considered brilliant. He was inclined to agree.

At twelve o'clock, Ben freshened himself up in his private washroom, the sole material difference he owned over his five colleagues, apart from the position of his office. He went out onto the gallery.

The next door opened and Harry Farnsworth appeared. He grinned, "Hello, old son."

"Hello, Harry."

"Haven't caught up with you in days."

Ben said, "I spend most of my time sleeping under my desk."

The other man laughed. In the early forties, he was balding and had a paunch; both showed more than they should because he had a tall man's stoop. His face was heavy, strong, vital, with dark hollows under the eyes. The eyes themselves were constantly on the move. You felt that after you had left him, he would not only be able to describe every detail of your person, but also what had been going on in the vicinity.

If Ben Armitage was thought brilliant, Harry Farnsworth was considered a genius. His job was safe for life.

"Nice to see you so cheerful nowadays," he said. "For a while back there, you were a miserable sod."

Ben shrugged. "So would you be if you ever tried to give up smoking." The lie came easily. "Withdrawal symptoms."

"It went on for months?"

"Try it, Harry."

"No, thanks," Farnsworth said. He lowered his voice and stepped closer. A confidence was coming. He said, "Talking of vices."

Ben nodded with acted tolerance. "Chorus girl? Go-go dancer? Model?"

"As a matter of fact, old son, she's a little mouse the average chap wouldn't look at twice. A case, you know, of hidden fires."

Ben asked abruptly, "How's Val?"

A look of annoyance showed for a moment in Farnsworth's eyes. Then he grinned. "You cheeky bastard. But you can't put me down that way."

"Wasn't trying to, Harry. I was wondering about Val."

"She's in top form, Ben, really top form. Come out to the cottage on Sunday. Drinks at noon. She'd love to see you."

"Thanks, but I'll be boating. Some other time, eh?"

"Of course. But listen. This mouse." Farnsworth took Ben's arm and walked with him along the gallery, the while talking in a low voice about the latest in a long line of extra-marital interests.

They parted at the top of the stairs. As Ben went down, wiping absently at the place on his sleeve that had been held by Harry Farnsworth, he thought it curious that, despite Harry's powers of observation, he hadn't noted that Ben had given up cigarettes years ago.

Outside, there was no exchange with the commissionaire, only his salute. That was part of the ritual. When Ben came back from lunch there would be, "Good afternoon to you, Mr. Armitage"—and "A good afternoon to you, Mr. Jeb."

Ben walked past the mouth of the garage. When he had

turned onto Threadneedle Street, he stopped and waited on the kerb until he was sure he was not being accidentally followed by anyone he knew. That settled, he went on at a brisker walk.

After turning several corners Ben began to watch out for a vacant cab. One soon came along. He waved it down, got in and said, "Trafalgar Square, please."

It was stifling in the taxi, the midday sun pouring down on roof and windows, so it didn't look odd when Ben took off his suit coat. In pleasing fact, the cabbie asked, "Warm enough for you, guv'nor?"

"Bloody right," Ben said. He undid his collar and pulled down the knot of his tie.

"Papers claim it's the hottest summer in sixteen years."

"For once I'll believe what they say."

"There you go."

As he left the taxi in the vast square, Ben slung his jacket over his shoulder casually. Now, he told himself, he looked like any other lunchtimer, indistinguishable from thousands. He wasn't sure he cared for that.

But, walking north, he aided the picture still further by buying a hot dog from a pushcart vendor. He made no attempt to taste the snack. It looked, he thought, unfit for human consumption. He nipped off the top inch and tossed it in the gutter, after which he fastidiously wiped his fingers on the paper napkin, and even that looked none too clean.

One hand hooking his jacket over his shoulder, the other holding the hot dog, Ben strolled into Leicester Square. He was among scores of office-freed loungers, most with sandwiches or ice creams, many hovering within hearing of the pop music that came from the penny arcade in one corner.

Reaching there, Ben went inside. Youths and slatternly girls who seemed afraid of showing pleasure were draping themselves around the pin-ball machines, one-arm bandits and other games. A man with an invalid pallor jiggled coins in the kangaroo pouch of his smock.

Nerves growing raw at the noise, Ben moved casually among the attractions. Two of them he tried. He failed to get a ball in the slot that would have given him his money back, just as he failed to reach a wristwatch with the claws of a crane.

Enough, he thought.

Above a descending stairway was a sign in neon that said Rifle Range This Way. More neon outlined a poor drawing of a girl in a bikini. The way she held a gun was pornographic.

Still casual, Ben crossed to the stairs and went down. He sighed with relief at leaving most of the blaring music behind. Excessive noise was one of his hates.

The basement held only the shooting gallery. Ten yards back from the counter and its canopy of light bulbs, were rows of clay pipes, Ping-pong balls abounce on jets of water and an endless line of white ducks that were pockmarked silver.

Leaning on the counter, pose insolent, was a girl of nineteen or twenty. Her fair hair draggled down from a dark parting. She wore white lipstick and her eyes were outlined starkly in black. Her jeans appeared tight enough to hurt, her large breasts were an inch away from being fully exposed.

There was no one else in the basement.

The girl pushed herself up sinuously. She asked, "Goin' to 'ave a go, sir?" The question had the stamp of repetition.

Cockneyfying his accent, Ben said, "I dunno. I never tried before. Is it easy?"

"Dead easy, mate," she said. His accent had removed the need for *sir*. "I'll show you the ropes. Nine shots for twenty-five pence. Okay?"

"Well, I dunno."

The girl pouted and swayed. So did her breasts. "You'll be a natural," she said. "I can tell by the look of you. Sure you never used a .22 before?"

"Sure," Ben said. He was lying. Last week he had gone to Hampstead Heath, where a travelling fair was pitched. There, for the first time in his life, he had shot a rifle. He had wanted to learn two things. First, could he handle the weapon; second, would he be able to stand that explosive report right beside his face.

The last point had soon been settled. Twenty-twos gave only a sharp crack, easily bearable. The first question, that had been undecided. He hadn't known whether he was doing it right or not, though he made no hits, and the stallholder was too busy to give him instructions.

"Come on, dear," the girl wheedled, "'ave a go."

Ben was not too pleased with the way she was scrutinising his face. He told himself he should have worn sunglasses. Putting down his jacket and hot dog, he said, "Okay then. You show me."

The girl positioned him in a lean on the counter. She placed a rifle in his hands, set its butt firmly against his shoulder. She put a hand on one of his, an arm around him, and pressed close.

"Now squeeze the trigger, dear," she crooned. "*Squeeze* it."

His start at the crack was mild. There was a following clang from somewhere among the targets.

"That wasn't too hard, was it, dear?"

"I didn't aim at nothing."

"We'll get to the aim now," the girl said. "Close your left eye."

Ben went on shooting. There was no need to reload. The breach fed itself automatically from the chamber that held nine bullets. With the eighth, he came close to hitting a clay pipe.

He eased up. The girl, not moving away, said, "Fantastic. I knew you 'ad the knack. For the very first, you did amazin' well."

"Thanks," Ben said. "It's a good gun."

"Only the best, mate."

"It seems a pretty dangerous weapon."

"I'll say. That's why you should learn your way around 'em."

"I'm surprised they're not illegal," Ben said.

"Naw. You can buy 'em anywhere. Don't even need a licence to own a .22. Now, how about another go?" Her breasts insinuated against his upper arm.

Ben, taken momentarily out of his concentration, mused: For God's sake, the bird fancies me.

That sexual blandishment was all part of the sales pitch would never have occurred to Ben, so long as he himself was involved. His mind didn't work that way.

In any case, he was not interested in the flashy girl, nor would he have been if he didn't need to be mindful of the lesson. He was no Harry Farnsworth.

"Okay, love," he said. "I'll have another bash."

"That's the way."

Taking turn after turn, Ben stayed at the rifle range for another half hour, until some youths came clattering down the stairs. He got an inordinate amount of triumph out of hitting the head of a clay pipe, his face reddening. He was mostly unconscious of the girl's body. He declined to have a try at a moving target because that wouldn't be needed. He felt, finally, that he had learned how to handle a gun reasonably well.

He went upstairs and out to the street. His hot dog he dropped into the first trash-can he passed. Out of Leicester Square he put his jacket on and slid his tie into place.

As he headed for a steak house on Coventry Street, he mused that all was going smoothly. He smiled and began to hum. The hum was quiet. The smile was quiet.

Some hours later, in an office block near Western Avenue, Jill Parr was wrapping up for the day. She stood by Mr. Olivieri's desk while he signed the letters she had typed. Her white blouse and straight skirt looked as fresh as when she had put them on that morning.

Mr. Olivieri finished reading a letter, signed it with a flourish, picked up another. He was a short, thin, middle-aged man whose expensive suit looked too big. His black hair, dense and wavy, had no grey at the temples. A hawk nose bullied the other features into insignificance, like shy doves. He wore a diamond ring on each hand.

Without looking up from his reading he asked, "Nice time on your birthday, Miss Parr?"

"Yes, thank you," Jill said. Recalling that her boss had already asked that question once today, she added, "And thanks again for the book token."

He brushed at the air as if shooing a fly, picked up another letter. "What did you do with yourself?"

"Shopping. A meal out. Movies in the evening with a friend. Very pleasant. A nice weekend altogether."

True, Jill thought. It had been fun. There had been no more nonsense after that business with the bottle of milk. The movie had been a lovely two-hanky deal. Best of all though, had been the long walk on Sunday afternoon, four times around Primrose Hill and then a detour back home.

"Yes, a good weekend," she said. She gazed through the window at the white-blue sky.

Mr. Olivieri signed the last letter. He shuffled them together and handed the sheaf over, smiling. "Boy friend, eh? The movies."

"No, sir. May Wilson. Her date stood her up at the last minute." Jill tried not to show her impatience. She wanted to be outdoors on this beautiful evening. She wished her Hillman's top hadn't deteriorated so badly that she daren't lower it for fear of not getting it up again. It would be great to drive with the top down.

"Pretty girl like you," Mr. Olivieri said. "I'm surprised you're not having to fight the men off with a sword."

"I'm past it, sir. Positively ancient. No one wants an old hag like me."

He gave a dry laugh, like a series of grunts. "Off you go, Miss Parr. See you tomorrow."

"Yes, sir. Good night."

Ten minutes later Jill was walking across the cindered car park. Another ten minutes and she was drawing near Chiswick. The car windows were down, her hair blew in the breeze. She felt wonderful.

Stop at the Royal Coach.

The thought came out of nowhere, suddenly. Jill tensed. She felt prickly under the arms. Her feeling of pleasure vanished. Not again, she thought. I don't like it.

But before worry could grow to strength, she saw ahead the swinging sign of the Royal Coach hotel. She told herself that she had known, of course, that she was approaching the pub— she passed it every day—and had thought it would be nice to stop there for a drink. It would keep her outdoors awhile longer on this super evening.

Jill also told herself that she didn't feel like a drink and that she never went in pubs alone. And if she did go in, that wasn't being outdoors.

She ignored both sides. "The heck with it," she said. "Home, James."

Stop here. Pull on the forecourt.

Jill winced. She found herself slowing the car. Her hands were gripping the wheel tightly. Her foot dithered back and forth between brake and accelerator.

"I won't," she mumbled, lifting her chin. "Damn it, I won't."

Now. Here. Turn in.

Jaw determined, Jill slammed her foot down on the power. The car trembled, groaned a complaint, but answered with a spurt of speed. She went by the forecourt entrance.

Jill's triumph lasted mere seconds. The urge to go to the pub, instead of fading now that she was past, grew stronger than before. Her face took on a look of sadness. She sighed, slowed the Hillman and turned into the next side street that appeared. Torpidly, she circled to the Royal Coach.

She pulled onto the fronting parking area and stopped between two other cars. After switching off the motor, she leaned back. She blinked, perking. The urge had gone.

The reason Jill got quickly out of the car and headed for the pub entrance, though she wasn't quite admitting this to herself, was to be doing it of her own choice before her mysterious, despotic subconscious came back.

She went in the lounge and over to the bar. Not long open for the evening session, the place had few customers. Jill still felt out of place, unescorted. I'm too damn old-fashioned, she thought.

At the counter she slid onto a stool. A barmaid came and smiled the question. Jill ordered a dry sherry. She got out cigarettes, having a strident need of the crutch, lit up and dragged smoke into her lungs.

The drink came. Jill paid, sipped. Feeling better, easier, she looked at her reflection in the bottle-backing mirror. She told herself she didn't look at all depraved.

Her gaze was diverted. She flicked it to the far end of the reflected scene. She had seen there something familiar. She stared hard, then swung head and shoulders to verify, to change from the image to the real. It was no mistake.

He sat at a table in the large bay window. He was reading a newspaper. At his elbow stood a glass of beer.

Slowly, a smile worked wonders on Jill's face. It was not

only on account of seeing the man. It was for the explained impulse that had brought her here.

Instinct, she mused. Good old female intuition. He must have mentioned once that he sometimes came to this pub in the evening. Or his car was outside, which fact hadn't been registered consciously.

Jill stubbed out her cigarette, picked up purse and sherry and got off the stool. She went over to the window table, stopped beside it and said,

"Well, look who's here."

Ben Armitage lifted his head quickly. He stared, grinned, began to get up. "Jill. Of all people. Marvellous. How nice to see you."

Jill said similar things as they shook hands and went through the niceties of greeting. She thought how well he looked, how sleek and confident.

They sat. Ben said, "You work near here, of course. Me, I come out this way once in a while to visit a friend of Dad's."

Jill felt a chaste obligation to say, "You never mentioned that." She also added, "I didn't see your car outside."

"I have a Jag now."

"Ah, the rich banker."

"No, the spendthrift."

They laughed, eyeing one another. Jill decided that Ben was much better looking than he had been three months ago. Then, he'd had a slump to his features and grim lines around his mouth. Furthermore, he had now lost that brooding manner which at times had been disconcerting.

Ben said, "I've often thought of you, Jill. But somehow I never got around to giving you a call. I've been so busy you wouldn't believe it."

The best answer was a smile and an understanding nod. Ben went on, "I've been constantly on the go, up and down the country. What a life."

They talked about their jobs. Jill finished her sherry. Ben signalled for a refill and another beer for himself. Jill felt more content than she had in weeks. She felt even better when Ben asked,

"How's the old love life, Jill?"

"Oh," she said casually, "jogging along."

"No steady?"

"At the moment, no."

Ben leaned forward. "Listen. How about coming for a run in the boat with me. Say Wednesday night."

"Why, Ben, that sounds lovely."

"We could have dinner at one of those little places along the river."

Jill didn't mind that she was blushing her pleasure because she had been told it suited her. She said, "Wonderful. I'd love to."

"Pick you up at your place at seven?"

"Perfect, Ben. Thanks."

He winked, leaned back and began talking about boating matters. Jill gave him half her mind while working busily on the problem of what she should wear for the river outing.

Presently Ben looked at his watch. "Sorry about this, but I have to gallop."

"Don't worry, so've I."

Outside among the cars, Ben squeezed Jill's hand and kissed her on the cheek. "Until Wednesday."

"Yes, Ben. 'Bye for now."

Jill went to her car. Inside, she found that her hands were slightly unsteady as she switched on the ignition. She smiled. She knew now what had been wrong with her lately, why she had been doing silly and near-dangerous things. Her life lacked romance and excitement. Had lacked, she thought.

Jill pulled out onto the road and drove on. She was happy.

The moment that Jill Parr's old convertible left the forecourt, Ben allowed the thrill to take over. He stood leaning back against his car, smiling, body loose. He felt fine and lofty.

Ben spared no thought for the fact that Jill had come over to his table of her own accord, or, again without control, had accepted the date. He took that for granted.

In any case, now that the girl had gone, Ben could hardly recall what she looked like.

He came alert, got in his Jaguar and drove out onto the road. He took the same direction as that of the Hillman. Although he wanted to race, keep time with his pleasure-keen nerves, he made himself hold to a steady speed.

He thought: Power. That's what it is. Power. The beauty and joy of command. It would be wonderful by itself, even without the other thing, the future. It was fabulous.

A faint tremor moved on Ben's smiling face. Excitement ran through him like tickly blood. He felt in much greater degree the way he always did when he stood on his balcony and surveyed the panorama of London.

Ahead of him on the road he saw Jill's Hillman. It came in and out of view beyond the traffic between. Ben had been about to pass the car in front of him. That might take him too close. He stayed behind.

He knew he shouldn't be here at all, should not have followed from the pub. He could be seen by Jill. But he was unable to resist trying for another command, gorging on that thrill. There would be more, lots more, but he wanted another one now, craved it the way a lung craves air.

Trouble was, Ben thought, it was impossible to concentrate hard enough while driving. The one time he had tried it, he'd nearly run into another car. The same when he was with Jill, or anyone else for that matter. Concentrating made him unaware of his surroundings.

The only hope now, therefore, of getting the thrill, was if Jill made a stop, so that he could stop as well.

Ben took in a deep breath through his smile. Allowing his excitement to ease to a simmer, he decided not to be greedy, not to strive for more. He could spoil everything if he pressed the matter for the sheer pleasure of it alone. And this evening had been good enough, great, sitting in the pub window and putting on the pressure as soon as the Hillman came into sight; thinking he'd failed, the car gone by, and then that marvellous burst of pride when two minutes later Jill had driven onto the forecourt. And Saturday. Well. Saturday.

Wearing a sailing cap and sunglasses, Ben had waited in his car near Jill's house. He knew she always shopped on Saturday mornings, starting around eleven. He also knew that he could change her mind should she decide otherwise. The rapport was still strong. It had not atrophied in three months.

The night before, Ben had stood watching her curtained window while thinking repeatedly, Look outside, Look outside. Only five minutes had passed before the drapes opened and Jill's face appeared.

On Saturday she came out of the house at eleven-fifteen. She drove away. Ben followed at a safe distance. He parked one block back from her in the West End. Following on foot, he had no definite plans. He would play it by situation.

The first came when he noticed the new Rolls-Royce. At once he went into deep concentration. It needed a lot of pressure before Jill responded, finally getting in the car. On alighting, she ran. He caught up on Oxford Street but then lost sight of her as she bustled into a store.

He wandered around the counters. He had given up, was on the point of leaving, when he saw Jill Parr again. They met almost face to face as she came out of a photo booth. He turned quickly and threaded along the crowded aisle.

Circling, he continued his discreet tailing as Jill left the store and windowshopped. He was not close enough to see any of the items she lingered over, therefore was unable to get to work.

The next opportunity came at a charity box. Jill was going to put a coin in. He made her put in a pound note instead. Since he knew she couldn't afford it, the thrill of accomplishment from that one was particularly fine.

Jill went upstairs to the cafeteria. Unable to risk going in, Ben stood outside and watched through the glass doors. Jill shared a table with an old man. Ben had a difficult time of coming up with what to make her do next. Throw food on the floor? Pull the man's beard? Tell him something outrageous?

The last were ruled out anyway: the man left. Ben went on thinking while watching Jill read a newspaper. He laughed aloud as he got the answer at last.

He had remembered that on one of their dates three months ago, dining in Soho, Jill had been embarrassed when he had complained, and mildly, about the quality of his steak.

He concentrated. The effect was immediate. Jill looked troubled. She fought hard, almost leaving, but gave in and went to report that her tea had been cold. Another fine thrill. And the danger was titillating as Jill, stark-faced, stalked toward the doors. He hustled to a radiator and squatted there as if doing a repair, his back turned.

Although he tailed her as closely as he dared down the stairs, she wasn't in sight when he got to the bottom. Obviously, he mused, she was in a panic. She had even dropped her chocolates.

After looking around inside and out, Ben realised that Jill could have gone home. He went along to where they had parked their cars. Hers had gone. Eager for a final trial, Ben drove to Jill's street. The Hillman was there.

He noticed in passing the house that one bottle of milk stood on the doorstep. Since, naturally, Jill would have taken her own milk in with her when she came back, the bottle must belong to one of the other tenants. This would be a wonderful test for prim and moral Miss Parr.

It took ten minutes of profound concentration before Ben saw the front door open, a slim hand sneak out and take in the bottle of milk. He drove away laughing.

Ben laughed again now, reliving that thrill from Saturday, the joy in power. It was not the laugh of amusement. It was the response of a hunter or an animal trainer. It held a certain amount of scorn.

Settling, driving along the busy rush-hour street, Ben wondered what Jill thought of these curious impulses she was getting. He supposed she would assume that her own mind was telling her what to do; it was the voice of her judgement. She might worry a little about the oddities, but it wouldn't hurt her to worry.

Ben had lost sight of the Hillman. He saw it again now—and he snapped alert. The car was parked. Jill had just got out and closed the door. Turning, she walked toward a bakery shop. If she were to glance around . . .

Ben couldn't stop; there was a truck right behind. He couldn't speed up; there were cars in front. He couldn't overtake; the approaching traffic was dense.

He drew closer. Jill paused by the shop door. Ben began to formulate excuses to explain why he was here, in case she turned and saw him.

But Jill went into the shop just as Ben came abreast. He blew out mightily. Next, relief turned to anger. He was furious with himself for being so careless, even though over a minor detail. The time for titillation had passed. The plan was firm. From now on, every step had to have meaning.

It was Harry Farnsworth who had taken Ben to the house in Hampstead. Ben had been unwilling. Harry had said, "As a favour. There's this young thing I'm seeing there. I told her I'd bring someone who knew all about black magic and so on."

"But I don't."

"Bluff it out, old son. Anyway, you might find it interesting."

Ben shrugged. "I doubt it."

"Cheer up, for God's sake. I don't know what's wrong with you lately. Val's right."

"Right about what?"

"She says you need a hobby."

"What rubbish," Ben said. "Okay, I'll help you out."

It was a cold February night when Ben and Harry Farnsworth called at the house in Hampstead. Admitted, they joined a thirty-strong group in the living room. All Ben knew was that these people, from various walks of life, gathered regularly to conduct tests in psychical research.

They look serious enough, he thought, gazing around from the corner he had found by the fire. The people ranged in age from late teens to the seventies. All were talking loudly and earnestly. Ben's only reaction was a mild disappointment that no one had an appearance of the exotic, mysterious or satanic. He prepared himself for boredom.

The talk was still going on when Harry Farnsworth came over with a huffed, "Stupid bitch. Can't think what I ever saw in her."

Ben wasn't surprised. This girl had lasted a fortnight, which was average. Farnsworth said, "I'm off. Are you coming or staying?"

"I might as well stay," Ben said, mostly because he felt thoroughly warm for the first time in hours. "At least for a while."

Harry Farnsworth snapped a nod and left.

Over the next half hour, until the group settled to business, several people came over to Ben and introduced themselves. They were merely being polite, he could tell. They weren't interested in outsiders. But he wondered why each gave him a close scrutiny when up close.

That was solved a few minutes later as he sat down and found himself beside a girl. They got into casual conversation. She said it was her first time here, and her last.

"I don't like spooky things. I came because May, my friend, she'll try anything once."

Ben said he was also a neophyte. The girl asked, "Did you get stared at too? They were looking for your aura. I haven't got one."

"Neither have I. I think it's all nonsense."

Then they and the other remaining talkers were shushed into silence. Everyone had moved to the sides of the room except for a couple, both sitting on the floor, their backs to each other and separated by three yards. The man had a pencil, the woman had five pieces of cardboard, which, Ben gathered, were called Zener cards. The object was for the man to note down his guess of which card the woman was concentrating on. The symbols were a cross, a triangle, a ring, a square, wavy lines.

Apart from calls from the couple, she that she was sending, he that he had received, the trial went on with everyone being totally silent. Ben knew he had been right to expect boredom.

A break came at last when the man's twenty guesses had to be checked. Talk arose. Ben said, "A yawner."

The girl nodded. "Yes, to watch. But it's interesting, this extra-sensory perception. And it's not spooky at all."

She was, Ben saw, fairly attractive, though not anything out of the ordinary. He said, "Why don't we sneak off, you and I? Have a drink somewhere."

She looked doubtful. "Well, I don't know."

He smiled. "I'm quite respectable. And my name's Ben Armitage."

"Jill Parr," she said. "Yes, okay. I'll just tell my friend."

Muffled in heavy coats they left the house and went to the
nearest bar. They had hot whisky toddies, also warm sausage
rolls. They talked about their jobs, homes, families, and
agreed it was hard to find a native Londoner in London.

Jill Parr said, "You know, we should try that game ourselves. The ESP thing. Shall we?"

"We haven't got the equipment."

Jill's answer was to go to a vacant table. It held a pack of
cards and a cribbage board. She brought the cards and set
aside the aces of each suit.

"There. That's good enough for us amateurs."

"Brilliant."

She held the four cards hidden in her hands. "Right. Now
see if you can guess which one I'm looking at."

Ben closed his eyes to help in thought. But no picture or
message came. He said, "I'll guess at a club."

"Wrong. Next one."

He was wrong ten times in a row. Indifferent to that, even
beginning to be indifferent to his companion, Ben took the
cards for his turn at sending. The top one was the ace of dia-
monds. He stared at it, letting it fill his vision, while simul-
taneously repeating its name in his head.

Jill, looking the other way, asked, "Er—diamond?"

"Yes. Very good. Go on." He held on to the same card.
Again Jill guessed right. She clapped. Ben told her to close her
eyes. She did so. He kept the same ace.

After a moment Jill said, "Sorry. I seem to be in a rut. I still
get a diamond."

"But you're right," Ben said. "A diamond it is."

"Honestly? You're not kidding?"

"Word of honour." He was no longer indifferent. He was
amused and intrigued. "Try the next one."

The game went on. Jill guessed right eight times out of ten.

She grinned like a tomboy. "Fantastic. I'm sure that must be a good percentage, aren't you?"

"Great percentage. Let's switch sides again."

They spent the rest of the evening until closing time passing the pack of cards back and forth. Ben was a consistent failure. But he felt that the roles of sender and receiver were equally important, and that he had a real talent as the former. Jill never scored below seven out of ten.

Before separating outside, they made a date to go to the pictures. It was not then but on their next date, dinner in a Soho restaurant, that Ben suggested they try more of the infant experiments in ESP. The reason for this was because he had been finding their conversation heavy going. He was not in the right frame of mind for romance.

They made the trial more complex. With Jill covering her eyes, Ben concentrated on one of the twenty-odd articles on the table. He was surprised when Jill said quickly, "Salt cellar." Though that was correct, Ben, out of nothing more than perversity, said, "No. Try again."

She did, and again she was right, guessing that he was sending a fork. This time Ben didn't lie. Over the following half hour he lied only when it suited him, which meant when he felt the girl had to be put in her place.

Jill never once guessed wrong. Ben was intrigued without the amusement. He didn't think, Clever Jill. He thought, Clever Ben.

"Let's try something even more difficult," Jill said. "After all, this could be coincidence or luck."

"Tell you what, see if you can guess the kind of car I was admiring in a showroom today. I'll think of it."

They both closed their eyes. Ben pictured the Jaguar he had coveted. He found it became clearer when he pressed fingertips to his temples. He concentrated hard.

Jill said, "A Daimler?"

He looked at her. "No, but you're not far off."

"Too bad. I got a picture of a fab red limousine."

Ben blinked. The Jaguar had been red. He said, "Let's get some coffee." The topic he changed to his speedboat.

Ben was vaguely disturbed. He felt now that there was something creepy about the girl's success—it seemed a mite better when he turned it around that way. It was like dabbling in black things you didn't understand. He decided on no more experiments.

During the rest of the evening, and on the drive to Cheever Street, Ben was moody and disinclined to talk. He wished he hadn't made a date to take the girl out on his boat.

When they were walking from car to house, Jill asked, "Truly now, tonight and in the Hampstead pub, did I guess right as often as you said?"

He shook his head. "No."

"I thought so. I knew you were only being nice to me. Who'd want to be psychic anyway?"

He kissed her lightly on the lips and turned away. "Good night."

"Night, Ben. See you on the river."

The sailing trip was not a success, not as far as Ben was concerned. Jill, however, seemed to enjoy herself. For Ben the outing was reduced from medium to poor by a return of that creepiness.

They were bobbing in the wash from a tourist launch. Angry because the larger boat had come too close in passing, Ben was telling himself to give it a blast on his siren. Go on, go on, he repeated in his emotional mind while reason was saying that the act would be pointless and petty.

Abruptly Jill leaned forward and pressed the horn button; after which, looking startled, she said, "Sorry. I don't know why I did it."

Afterwards, standing with her by the Hillman, Ben said,

"I'm going up to Leeds for a week or so. I'll call you when I get back."

"Fine, Ben. I'll look forward to that."

He left and returned to his speedboat. He never expected to see Jill Parr again.

Jill finally decided on sneakers, white jeans, a skinny sweater in light blue, and with a cardigan taken along in case the night grew chilly. The outfit had reached settlement after a two-hour discussion on the telephone with May Wilson.

The evening was warm, the mid-week river quiet. Ben, humming, cruised at a steady speed. Jill reclined luxuriously on the white leather seat and let one hand trail in the water. Her sole regret was that water-trailing a hand was trite. It felt good enough to make her think she had just discovered it.

Jill was much more at ease than on her first boating trip with Ben, months ago. Mainly this was because of Ben himself. As on their accidental meeting in the Royal Coach, he was relaxed. Although not the type for laughter, hearty or otherwise, he smiled a lot. There was quiet confidence in the smile.

Jill lit a cigarette. She said, "I'll bet you've recently climbed another step at Waringford and Myer."

He shook his head. "Nope. Still number two in Domestic."

"Number two tries harder."

Ben nodded slowly, thoughtfully. After a moment he said, "That's probably my problem. I've never had to try. It always came so easily to me. There's no challenge. That's why I'm not interested in my work."

"Really?"

"Really. Though Harry'd have a fit if he knew that. He's number one. I'm his protégé, in a way. He's been steering me through the other climbers. I've got what they haven't, he says.

It's what he calls a rapier mind. I've never found that particularly flattering."

"Oh, I don't know," Jill said. She herself was flattered. It was good that Ben was being so honest with her about his job. Although, she had to admit, he was talking in an abstracted way, more to himself than to her.

"Yes," Ben said, "Harry wouldn't be at all pleased to know I have no intentions of spending my life in banking, at Waringford and Myer or anywhere else. I'm no nine-to-fiver. That's no way for a man to live."

"Ben, with you it's more like ten to four."

As if he hadn't heard, he went on, "I don't see me growing old in this country or in this part of the world. Europe's had it. The path ahead is down. Asia, that's one place with a future. Everything's going to happen there. Or South America. Peru's only just coming out of its long sleep. New Zealand, the Canadian Northwest. Anywhere you look away from soiled old Europe there's vitality and potential."

Ben looked around, sat straighter, shuffled himself. "Sorry about that," he said. "I do ramble on sometimes."

Jill was not sure, but she had the impression that he was irked with himself, as if he had told her something improper. She said, "It's fun to hear someone talk ambitiously."

"Stupidly, most would say. But enough of that. Seen any good films lately?"

Jill told of the weepy. She thought it wise to add, "I went with my friend May."

Ben said, "There's a new thriller at Marble Arch. Would you like to go? Saturday?"

"Love it madly. So long as you hold my hand if I get scared."

"Right," he said. "Now let's see if we can coax some speed out of this fancy thing."

Near Kingston they drew in to the bank. From there, sloping up to a whitewashed pub, was a lawn scattered with rustic furniture. People were dining and drinking. It was a pretty scene, if slightly unbelievable.

Jill ordered the same as Ben, mixed grill. She was surprised at her order, since, though no vegetarian, she was not much given to meats, especially in quantity. She mused without reprimand that she was trying to make herself as amenable as possible.

You will enjoy this, she thought, looking down at the plate that held steak, a chop, two sausages, kidneys and a piece of liver. Enjoy it she did, helping herself to the French bread and rosé wine, though afterwards she felt queasy. That she cured with three cups of coffee.

During the meal, Ben referred only once to his work. He said, "Lucky you. I have a conference Saturday morning. I suppose you'll be out shopping."

"Probably."

"By the by, if you go to Cartway's, you might notice for me if they're having a sale in the men's department."

Amenable again, Jill, instead of saying she rarely went as far as Kensington, said, "Yes, I'll check in Cartway's for you."

"Thanks."

They went back in darkness and twinkling lights, Jill sitting close with an arm around Ben's back. Their silence was comfortable.

From the mooring they drove in the Jaguar to Cheever Street. Ben parked and killed the motor. Jill moved into his arms. They kissed. She murmured, "If you want to come in for a nightcap . . ."

"Another time," Ben said. "There's paperwork waiting at home." He kissed her again.

His manner, Jill thought, was restrained. She next thought what a fool she was. If a date rushed to the grope she got an-

noyed, and she was the same if he treated her with respect.
Talk about inconsistent.

Over the following days Jill was cheerful. She acted less
sternly efficient at work, and at home went up twice to keep
Miss Kelly company. She was visited by no more of those curious impulses. It made for additional pleasure that, for a change,
she was looking forward to the weekend.

Saturday morning, when Jill was getting ready to go out, it
occurred to her that she should wear a raincoat. Too hot, she
mused. But she became convinced that to go out without a
coat would be stupid.

She went to the window, looked up at the sky. There were
few clouds in the clear blueness. Even so, Jill concluded, she
should definitely put on her lightweight raincoat because you
just never knew with English weather.

She drove to Kensington and parked in the multi-story garage adjoining Cartway's, the store that boasted it could supply everything from a pin to a porpoise. Inside, courtesy of the
air-conditioning, Jill soon cooled from the heat caused by her
coat.

First, she went to the men's department. There was no sale.
Next she set off for the elevators. Mentally she ticked off the
items she wanted: pantyhose, skin moistener, green thread, a
scarf or blouse to settle that birthday gift problem. All could
be got on the third floor, above.

She stood by the line of elevators. The door of the nearest
slid back and its operator said, "Going up."

Jill found herself shaking her head. Surprised, she turned
away. Her surprise turned to worry. Was this another of those
silly urges? If so, what was the urge?

Downstairs.

Solemn, refusing to think about it, Jill walked to the escala-
tors. Her hands, inside the raincoat pockets, were clenched

into tight fists. She got on the moving stairway and went down to the basement.

It was totally given over to sporting goods. Jill began to move among the stands and counters. Her fists gradually relaxed as she felt no particular impulse, only the desire to be here, and to keep moving.

She went past tents, folding furniture, knapsacks, fishing equipment. She saw dummies in wetsuits, tracksuits, mountaineering gear, football uniform. There was nothing she found of interest. Furthermore, she didn't like the strong odour of leather.

There.

The thought, commanding, came almost as a relief. At least she would soon know what her worry was all about.

Jill came to a stop. She was by the end of a shop-type counter. Behind it, a clerk was leaning over in earnest conversation with a youngish couple who were accompanied by a child. The centre of interest was an imitation duck.

Jill looked down beside her. Leaning on a trestle stand were a dozen rifles. She stared at them wonderingly for a moment, then jerked her eyes away.

Although wanting to move on, she felt too weak to do so. She stared as if asking for help at the people at the counter. The duck was no toy, but a life-like copy in grey and white.

Take a rifle.

Jill twitched. She lifted her chin. That didn't keep her eyes from going back down to the gun-rack. She told herself feebly that it wasn't a bad idea to take a gun over to the salesman and ask for details on price and type and so on, and then see about getting one for her father next Christmas.

Jill's head angled down. She moved one step closer to the rack. The first in the row of guns was eighteen inches away, within easy reach.

Take a rifle. That one. No one's looking.

Jill tried to ignore the thoughts by tuning to others. But none would come. She was even unable to cogitate, as previously, on the reason behind those of command. They were too strong.

Sweat coated her top lip and slimed the insides of her clenched hands. She was unconsciously nodding in agreement while thinking that it would be a simple matter to reach out with her left hand; get hold of that rifle by its barrel; lift it and bring it to her; push it beneath the right side of her coat, which was unbuttoned; clamp her arm down on the gun; turn and walk slowly away.

Simple. As easy as could be.

But this is absurd, the most ridiculous . . . the . . .

Her thought died away, replaced by another that told her she had to be careful, to make sure she was not observed, to be smart.

Jill's eyes took on a cast of craftiness. She looked at the counter. All clear there. She looked behind. Two men were twenty feet away, examining a football. They were rapt.

Jill brought her left hand out of the pocket and stealthily reached it forward.

"Can I help you?"

She started and jerked her head around. Beside her was the salesclerk. She was aware unsteadily of a thin face, a black jacket, clasped hands.

You are only browsing.

"I'm only browsing," Jill whispered. Her hand was still out, poised in air. She brought it back.

The clerk tilted his head. "Ma'am?"

Jill cleared her throat. In a louder voice she said, "I'm just looking around. Thank you."

He smiled, veered grip and head toward each other in a form of bow, turned and went back to the couple. The three again gave their attention to the wooden duck.

All is clear. The men have gone.

Jill glanced behind. It was true. The two men were no longer there. With a faint wonder at how she could have known that, Jill looked back and again put out her hand.

She touched the barrel, grasped it. She lifted. The rifle was heavier than expected. It brought her onto her toes as she drew it from the stand and toward herself.

After that first directing look on reaching out, Jill had kept her eyes on the three people at the counter. They were engrossed. She went on watching them as she put the rifle inside her coat, the barrel tip near her armpit.

The thicker, middle part of the weapon she gripped with her pocketed right hand. The load felt insecure. She kept hold of the barrel with her left hand.

The salesclerk glanced around, paused, looked away again.

Leave. Nothing to wait for.

Jill turned. She turned and stopped. Six feet away, a boy was watching her fixedly. She recalled that there had been a child with the couple. This one. He was about six years old, and by his stance and eyes she knew he had seen everything.

Leave.

Jill moved. She began to walk. The boy stared at her and she stared at the boy. Then she had to break off the connexion because she was angling away. A moment later, she glanced back.

The boy was running to his parents.

Jill bumped into someone. She halted, flurried. The someone was a fat woman. She said a cold, "Really."

Jill was unable to speak. But she came close to crying out as the woman, brushing roughly past, almost knocked the rifle out of her hands.

Jill was gaping and her eyes were sad. She stood there. Her hands held on to the gun tightly. She looked behind. The boy was tugging at his father's coat and pointing toward Jill.

Leave, leave, leave.

She moved on. One step, two steps, three steps; each was a journey. She doubted she would ever reach the high display stand that would put her out of sight of the counter. But she did. She reached and rounded it and was then able to walk faster. The expected shout from behind didn't come.

Jill was at the escalator. She got on. She felt like running up but there were two hefty schoolgirls in front of her, side by side. She stood and suffered the slow ascent.

Her feelings, Jill realised with a start, had changed. It was as though water had been dashed in her face to bring her out of a reverie. It came to her now, the full and fantastic implication of what she had done, was still doing. She could hardly believe it. Yet the rifle was there under her coat and solid in her hands.

She was a thief. Any minute now they would catch up with her and she would be arrested.

Jill was appalled at herself and terrified of the consequences. Not noticing that the escalator was at the top, she stumbled over the unmoving ridges. Fear made her look back. No one on the stairway seemed to be in a hurry.

She went on. She told herself not to show haste. Obeying, she moved at an ordinary pace along the aisle. Several shoppers looked at her, at the oddness of her down-clamped right arm and the partly hidden left.

Marvelling at her ability to act in a normal manner, Jill went through the doorway that led to the garage. In the dimness there, she ran to her car and opened the door. The area was free of people. She brought out the gun, dropped it behind the front seat, got behind the wheel and slammed herself in.

Five minutes later, short-cutting through Hyde Park, she pulled into the side and stopped. She put both hands to her face. "I won't cry," she said. "I won't cry."

The next time Jill stopped, it was in Cheever Street. She switched off and sat leaning forward on the steering wheel. Her eyes were red.

The train of her drear musing was running along lines of disgrace, prison, parental shock and sorrow, when the idea came to her that she could leave it until after dark. She drew upright, wondering, Leave what?

At once she realised that she meant, of course, the rifle. It would be madness to carry it from the car in broad daylight. She should leave it here and come back for it later.

Jill got out of her Hillman and walked swiftly to the house, her head lowered. For a moment there at the wheel, she had felt as when taking the gun—weak. Now she felt her normal self again; and again was in despair.

In the flat she threw off her raincoat. She let it fall to the floor. She began to pace, hands rubbing each other as if chilled. Twice she moved out of the circle she was describing, once to lock the door, once to draw the curtains. Her mind was consumed with worry but not thought. She dwelled on possibilities, the terrible ifs.

An hour passed before Jill made herself sit down in the kitchen with coffee and a cigarette; sit down and say, "Right. Now. I've got to think about this."

She tried. But it was odd, thinking about thinking. She felt strange. She was not, she knew, the type for ratiocination. Often she would come alert from a rest or a stroll and realise she had been musing on absolutely nothing. That's why she liked company. That's why she talked to herself: it was company's cousin.

And these thoughts that came when she did weird things. They were peculiar. For instance, when one decides to make coffee, one doesn't think I WILL MAKE A CUP OF COFFEE. It comes as a collection of ideas mixed with a physical want, not

as a procession of words in the mind. But that was how it had
been during her crazy doings.

It was, Jill supposed, a way of talking to yourself. You
could do that aloud at home, but not if there were people
around. So you did it in your head.

But why the crazy things? Well, she'd always heard that old
maids and people who lived alone went a bit odd. She did live
alone but she was no old maid, and . . .

Kleptomania. Now that was something. That could be it.
She'd wanted to steal the Rolls-Royce, she'd wanted to steal
the milk, she *had* stolen the gun. The other capers, they could
be as she had reasoned them afterwards. Yes, kleptomania. It
was so common that it was almost respectable.

Jill resettled herself on the chair, gulped coffee, took a deep,
fast, hissing draw on her cigarette. She warmed to the idea by
remembering that kleptomaniacs always took things they had
no material use for. And what use did she have for a Rolls-
Royce, a bottle of milk and a rifle? But there was a psychological connexion between things taken by compulsive thieves;
what possible connexion could there be between a car, milk
and a gun?

Jill almost smiled. Yet she held onto the restful idea. She
also, pouring more coffee, accepted that there was no danger
of her being caught for today's theft.

That led to a realisation that brought more cheer. She could
pay for the rifle. Later, she would buy a money order for the
amount on the price tag and send it to Salesman, Gun Dept,
with a note explaining that the theft had been done on a dare.
Perfect.

She went back to the main room, coffee in hand. The curtains she pulled back. And maybe, she thought, the whole
problem was that the business girl was frustrated. She no
longer wanted a career. She wanted to be a wife and mother.
So perhaps if, say, Ben Armitage showed more interest, inter-

est of a serious nature, the nonsense would end. And she was seeing Ben tonight.

Jill finished her coffee quickly and went to the bathroom to bathe her eyes.

On Monday afternoon Ben was leaning on the gallery rail in the bank. He watched the scene below. Two clerks were loading boxes of cash onto a trolley. Beside it stood three security guards, who would take it out to the armoured truck waiting behind the building. Another clerk was keeping tally.

Ben automatically kept it with him, knowing how much each box contained. The total came to a hundred and forty thousand pounds.

Ben looked at his watch, looked down again as the loading clerks started bringing sacks of coins. All the money was handled with the disdain that banking people hold for the real as opposed to the abstract.

A hand clamped down on Ben's shoulder. His nerves jerked him into a turn. Grinning at him was Harry Farnsworth, a bundle of papers under his arm.

He said, "Got you."

"Mm?"

"So this is how you waste the time of Waringford and Myer, is it?"

Ben snorted. "Stuff 'em," he said. "I've just earned the bank a fortune with one short phone call."

"Those film people?"

"Right."

Farnsworth nodded knowingly. "That's where you shine, old son. You keep up. I take it then that ghost movies are the in thing at the moment."

"Never really been out, Harry. They're a good bet."

"Talking of ghosties and ghoulies and things that go bump in the night. What ever happened to that mind-reader?"

Ben felt himself tensing. "Who?"

"That girl you met at the Hampstead freaks' nest we went to a few months ago. You remember."

Ben didn't. He did not, that is, recall telling Harry about Jill Parr. But he relaxed on realising that it had no significance. "I vaguely remember the girl," he said. "Never saw her again."

He looked at his watch. "Will you scream if I leave even earlier today?"

"Date?"

"No, the old man. I had a letter from him this morning."

After nodding his understanding/permission, Harry Farnsworth said, "Thursday, seven o'clock. We're having a few people in for drinks. You have to come. Val would love to see you, I know."

"I'll try," Ben said, moving away.

"It's an order. You can't leave early today if you refuse to accept."

"Balls." Ben opened the door of his office. "I'll be there."

"Good man."

Sitting at his desk, Ben took an envelope from his pocket, tore it up and threw it in the waste basket. Such letters came from his father at regular intervals. They complained of a widower's loneliness and hinted with a growing lack of subtlety that parent should be invited to share the home of son.

The notion filled Ben with depression. He had never been close to his father and mother, whom he had seen on only a dozen or so weekends a year. They had travelled the country selling a furniture polish of their own manufacture.

Ben's answer to the letters of whimper always took the same form. He would go to his old home without delay and joke his father into a better humour. Half the time, spacing to allay suspicion, he would pretend he had received no letter, had come down on the spur of the moment.

Ben left the bank at three-thirty. Traffic was heavy in the

south-west direction of Portsmouth. Ben had to spurt and crawl. Today, he was unconcerned.

He had not fallen into the usual slough on getting his father's letter, so was in no tearing hurry. The crest of good fortune he was on, he felt, could not easily be broken. Staying in his traffic lane, Ben mused happily on how matters were developing.

Saturday morning had gone perfectly. Jill had the gun. It had been a brilliant move, asking her to check in the men's section. That cancelled the need for riskily tailing her from Cheever Street. There, all he'd had to do was wait to see if she had obeyed the order to wear a coat; then drive straight to Cartway's and wait to pick up her trail in men's wear.

Later, mission accomplished, he had gone to Cheever Street fast, parked around the corner, and when Jill showed up told her what to do about the rifle—the dumb bitch was liable to take it out of the car there and then.

Saturday night Jill had looked peaked. Obviously she was worried. There was danger in that, the human element which all plans had to take into consideration. She might tell everything to her doctor, a friend, a psychiatrist. But it was doubtful. Proper little Jill would be too full of guilt.

On their date Ben had given Jill no tests. He needed to be careful about too many orders while in her company, didn't want her to connect them with him. Even so, she had picked up some of his thoughts on her own account. The rapport was growing stronger.

Ben hummed quietly as he drove.

It was still daylight as he reached his old home. The house stood in a suburb with mingled attributes: small factories next to poultry farmlets, houses next to market gardens. The sides of most properties carried billboards.

Ben noted that the Armitage house now bore a painting of a smiling baby, one eye disfigured by the lavatory window. As

far back as he could recall, that facade had proclaimed itself
to be the home of Armitage's Superior Polish.

After his mother's death, Ben had advised his father to give
up travelling. He had done so. Instead, he advertised in pro-
vincial newspapers.

"I'm still making a living, lad," he said, as with a hard grip
on Ben's elbow he brought him into the house. "Can't complain about money."

"That's good, Dad."

"But it's time I quit. I'm getting on, you know."

Mr. Armitage was an older version of Ben, with the plumpness given up being a mere tendency, the eyes pale, and the
curly hair turned bracken grey.

"You're only sixty-two," Ben said.

"It ages a man though, being alone. I believe I mentioned it
in my letter."

"What letter's that, Dad?"

The evening followed the pattern. Ben talked about how
great it was to be free of London, which wasn't fit to live in,
but his job was there; about how lucky his father was to be his
own boss, and without ties; about how older men he knew of
had got married again or emigrated.

Ben mentioned several times that the house was looking
clean and tidy—and mused that it had never been so during the
years it was taken care of by the series of housekeeper-foster-
mothers.

He laughed at each of the stale, unfunny anecdotes from
travelling days, said you never heard stuff like that in London,
which wasn't fit to live in. He produced the whisky he had
brought and they finished it before midnight. He went to his
room feeling fine.

In bed Ben was restless. The alcohol had agitated his
nerves, sharpened his perceptions. Sitting up, he put the light
on again and looked around his old room. It held all his books

and toys. He began to think of that boy he had known so well and now had almost forgotten.

Abruptly, Ben remembered other sleepless nights here. There had been many. Hundreds, it seemed. Ben recalled why he hadn't slept on those nights. He had been wishing his parents home, *willing* them to come back at once.

Hours had been spent concentrating, whitened knuckles to his temples. He would picture his parents as they drove. He would have them say, "Let's go back and see if our boy's all right." He would see them arrive and embrace him, and listen sympathetically to the story of wrongs done by the current housekeeper, who would then be chastised.

Ben remembered the countless mornings when he had got up and gone confidently along to his parents' room and been astonished to find it still empty, their return not having happened.

At other times during the wakeful, lonely nights he would evoke his mother's face, searchingly examine her eyes, while thinking, "I'm hurt, Mummy. Help me. I'm in trouble. Mummy, come quickly. Come and save me."

He would think this so hard and so long that his head ached. There were useful results, but when his parents did return, his mother would run a hand over his hair and ask, "Been all right?"

A rotten childhood, Ben thought. He put out the light and went to sleep.

He got up at seven. His father came downstairs as well, a topcoat over his pajamas. He made toast and tea. It was the pattern again. Ben said how much good it did him to get away from the same faces he saw every day, to leave London, to hear some solid talk, he must try to do it more often.

Armitage senior walked with Ben to the car, walked beside it with a hand on the windowsill as Ben backed out onto the

road, and walked a few paces in the same direction as Ben
drove off.

Jill was getting ready for her date. After putting on a peasant skirt, pleased that its waist was no more snug than last
time, she reached in among the hanging clothes for a blouse.
She saw, and looked away from, the rifle. It was propped in a
corner of the wardrobe.

As she put the blouse on, her sole thought in respect of the
gun was a positive: she was glad she had mailed off that
money order, along with an unsigned block-letter note of explanation.

The bedroom being too small to hold a vanity table, Jill
took her brush to the bathroom. She looked in the mirror and
counted aloud while giving her hair its daily one hundred
strokes. Doing it now, A, made her hair shine and float for
going out, and B, saved her having to face the chore when she
got home tired.

Jill ignored the fact that whenever she did brush her hair
post-outing, she always cheated, jumping from fifty to seventy.

". . . eleven, twelve, thirteen," she said. "I'll wash it tomorrow. Fourteen, fifteen, sixteen. Weds were always hair nights
at home. Seventeen, eighteen . . ."

Jill was cheerful. Ever since Saturday she had been speaking to herself aloud instead of internally. Which fact made her
wonder—pause in brushing—if her theory on that had been the
reason for the cessation. Sort of uncover the cause, kill the
effect. Yet she was reminded that this had also happened last
week; the oddness had been only on Saturday. Well, more or
less. Perhaps—

But Jill was sick of the whole business, sick and tired of
questions and answers. She went on with the brushing,
quickly, snapping out numbers like an auctioneer.

She was ready to go, idly flipping through a magazine, when

she heard the distinctive Jaguar horn-blast. Going out, she tripped lightly and happily downstairs.

Ben, in the driver's seat, was leaning across with the door pushed open. Jill was glad they had passed beyond that polite stage, him seeing her in and out of the car. It was a nuisance after the first couple of times. Also, it seemed to imply a lack of intimacy.

"Hello, Jill. You look very pretty."

"Thank you, sir. You're very smart yourself." He was wearing a safari jacket and foulard. "Are we going to the jungle?"

He grinned. "Darkest Middlesex. Hold tight."

They shot away from the kerb. Fifteen minutes later they turned onto the M1 motorway. The speedometer needle went dithering past the hundred mark.

Jill found the speed exhilarating. Ben felt the same, she could tell. His new-found, confident smile was there in full force and his eyes had a happy narrowness. She liked to see him this way, boyish and eager.

Jill wondered what problem, if any, had made him so apt to fall into moody periods when she had first met him. Whatever —health, domestic, financial—it was obviously a thing of the past.

At length they pulled off the motorway. The country roads were quiet, but too erratic for speed. Ben slowed to thirty. It felt like walking. Jill was able to enjoy the lush scenery and have no fears of dangerously diverting Ben's attention with talk.

They stopped at a pub. Its parking area was full of cars and motorcycles. "Meanwhile," Jill said, "the locals are packing the London bars."

Inside, the crowd was dense. It was several minutes before Ben could get served. He got two tall Pimm's. Jill followed out to the garden behind. It was large, with low-hanging trees and as many people as inside.

Jill and Ben found a vacant table on the edge. As they sat, a group of folk singers began performing. They were amateurs but had a rough, naïve style that was refreshing. The performance lasted an hour. Between sets, Jill and Ben chatted. It was developing into the kind of restful evening Jill had hoped for.

Dusk came, then dark. Lanterns in the branches above came on softly. Many tables emptied as people moved inside to the community singing. Ben fetched the third round of Pimm's, along with two thick slices of ham and egg pie.

Snack over, Ben and Jill drew their chairs closer together. Ben put his arm around her shoulders. They kissed languidly. Their corner was dim and the garden had few people left now, and those were mostly self-concerned couples like themselves.

Ben drew back. He reached for his glass. Jill left hers alone because she was feeling the effects of the innocent-tasting but potent drink. She got out her cigarettes.

Ben finished his Pimm's, got up and strolled to a nearby table. Jill watched in growing surprise as he lifted an empty beer glass, pint size, the heavy mug-type with a handle and dimpled sides. Not hurrying, Ben put the glass into one of the large pockets of his safari jacket. Jill blinked slowly, her cigarette held unlit, forgotten.

Ben moved on. He strolled to the far end of the garden, came back, the while gazing up and around at the lanterns. His manner was perfectly normal, casual.

He arrived at the table from which he had started. Again with no furtiveness, he brought the beer glass from his pocket and put it down. He came back to his chair.

Jill said, "What on earth were—"

Ben interrupted with a sudden, "Hey, there's John Leicester. God's sake." He began to get up. "'Scuse me, Jill. Be right back. That's someone I know."

He strode quickly away and went from view around a corner of the building. Jill, bemused, gave a short laugh. She lit her cigarette and wondered what could possibly have been the reason for that thing with the glass.

A mistake.

Oh dear. She was talking to herself inside again. What a bore. "I'm tight," Jill said aloud.

He didn't take the glass. You imagined it. You thought you saw him put it in his pocket and then return it. A mistake. It was your imagination. You were thinking of yourself and the rifle. You want others to do the same sort of thing.

Smoking in quick puffs, Jill sat and listened to her interior monologue. Her feet were pressed hard against the grass. She supposed that yes, she could have imagined the whole scene. It was dim here. She had been drinking. He might simply have lifted the beer glass, looked at it and put it down again. Guilt could have done the rest.

And she was still talking to herself inside. That stopped as Ben appeared from around the corner. He was smiling, though with rue rather than cheer. It had that slant.

"That was awkward," he said, sitting. "I thought it was someone I knew, gave him a great slap on the back. Turned out to be a total stranger. He laughed, of course. But still."

"Ben?"

"Yes?"

No, she thought, it had all been imagined. She would look crazy if she asked him about it. Jill said, "Nothing."

Ben was standing on his balcony. The sinking sun lit sparks on a thousand windows across London. The view was magnificent. Ben saw none of it. He was nervous. Today was Thursday.

He knew he should leave but had an understandable reluctance. For the tenth time he took in and threw out again the idea of telephoning to say he couldn't make it. An excuse would be easy enough to find, sure, but there had been too many lately. He had to go. He had to bear it.

Swinging around, Ben went inside his slick modern living room, all chrome tubing and red leather. He headed for the miniature bar in one corner, changed his mind halfway, went into his bedroom and got a tranquiliser. Perversely denying himself water—he shouldn't have agreed to attend the party in the first place—he chewed on the pill as he left his flat and went down in the lift.

He used more delaying tactics in getting in his car and during the drive. It took him a third as long as usual to get to the open country in the Cranwell area.

Turning onto a back lane, Ben's tension eased. Now when he slowed the Jaguar it was not a delaying ploy. He looked at the fork junction he was approaching. He knew ever detail.

On the point where the lane split, stood a red telephone box. Behind that rose a high clump of bushes. All around were trees. There was no sign of a house.

Ben drove on. His moment of confidence passed and he became tense again. He took the right-hand fork.

At the sides of the lane were tangly hedges of bramble. On the left appeared a huge, ancient oak. It leaned over the lane like a friendly monster. Eighty feet beyond that, a white gate stood open. Ben drove in.

After a short run between trees he came to the cottage. On the gravel turnabout were half a dozen cars, all newish, all expensive. Ben parked and got out.

Postponing again, he stood and looked at the house. It was Georgian, two stories of red brick and white trim. It was simple, unpretentious—and, with its two acres of land, worth a fortune.

Ben forgot delay as he gazed at the house and at the cars. He thought about money. He thought what a paltry ambition it was to have it, use it, show it. These people, they were so sold on the material things of life, the way he pretended to be himself, that they didn't know how to enjoy, say, a sunset, unless they'd had to pay to see it.

What, Ben mused, was this mad striving, clawing yearn for gold? What insanity was it that drove executives, adventurers, robbers, embezzlers to ruin their health and risk their lives and endanger their freedom? Far better for a man to have enough to get by on in comfort, living in an easy-going part of the world. He wouldn't need wealth. All he needed was the right woman.

Ben's nerves became taut again. He felt like leaving. Surmounting that, he went over to the cottage. The front door was open. Ben entered the small hallway, stairs climbing on one side. Through the kitchen door on the left, Ben could see a woman, the evening's hired help.

She looked around and nodded. "Hello there, Mr. Armitage."

He managed a smile. "Maggie."

"What weather."

"Beautiful," he said. He knew that, as Maggie loved to talk, he could linger here another ten minutes. It was pointless. He turned to his right and opened the living room door.

There were fifteen or so people, with a handful more visible through French windows at the room's far end. The dress was casual, the age bracket enclosed forty. The noise level would have sufficed for twice as many people. The party had been going on for some time.

Harry Farnsworth came forward. He was flushed and smirky. "Thought you weren't going to make it," he said. "You look disgustingly sober."

"Well, I'm not. I stopped on the way and had a couple with a cute little barmaid."

It was the right drift for Harry Farnsworth. He pulled a floppy mouth of appreciation. "Nice bit, eh?"

"Luscious. I'm keeping this one to myself."

"Pig."

It occurred to Ben for the first time—and he was surprised at not having thought of it before—that like many men who continually harped on sex and loved to tell dirty jokes, Harry could be impotent, or close to it. Ben liked the idea.

The host said, "You know where the booze is, old son. Get a drink and circulate. Val's outside. See you." He moved off.

Ben went to the drinks table. Standing there was a woman he knew. He listened to her talk of the fabulous weather while fixing himself a weak Scotch and thinking about his new idea in respect of Harry Farnsworth's virility. By the time Ben had taken the first sip of his drink, doubt in the matter had gone. Ben had decided. Harry was impotent. It made everything so much easier to bear.

The woman was still talking as Ben patted her shoulder and moved on. He stopped twice to exchange greetings with acquaintances while working his way to the end of the room. He stopped again to form a triangle with two men. They said hello briefly and went on with their talk of politics.

Ben looked between them at the French windows. His stomach felt empty.

Val Farnsworth was talking to a woman of about her own age, thirty. They were the kids of the crowd. They didn't like each other, and it showed in the way their eyes projected affection. Ben didn't see the other woman. Val could have been talking to a horse for all he knew.

Harry's wife was medium height and slim. She stood not straight but in a wavy line, one hip out, which pose she reversed frequently as a part of verbalising the way some people use gestures. Her hands, crossed at the wrists behind her back, fluttered like a bird's wings.

Val wore a short black skirt, a white blouse. Her calves were as roundly, smoothly noticeable as her hips and breasts.

She had a light tan. Her face was pretty reaching for beautiful. Her jaw was too strong for the ultimate. Even so, it had a petiteness, the face, a waif quality that was accentuated by the urchin haircut and large anxious eyes.

Without warning, she turned and looked directly at Ben. His vacuum of a stomach lurched. Just as abruptly, Val Farnsworth looked back at her companion. Ben went on watching. He was like a pauper outside a bakery.

One of the men spoke to him. He answered, though wasn't sure of what he said. He came fully alert when he realised that both men were looking at him oddly. He must have replied in the wrong tack. He didn't care. Nodding he turned away, drained his glass and went to the drinks table.

Glass refilled, he was raising it when he felt and saw the tanned hand come to rest on his arm. Feebly putting down his drink he lowered his head as Val Farnsworth stretched up to kiss his cheek.

"Ben, you've been neglecting us."

"I see Harry every day." His voice was unsteady. His eyes were roving the woman's face. It occurred to him in swift passing the superiority of this unpainted face to such cosmetic masks as Jill Parr's.

"Me, then," Val said. "You could've come last Sunday at noon."

A long moment passed before Ben answered. Then he said, "It hurts."

Harry's wife flicked a glance around at the others. Ben put a hand on hers, which still rested on his arm. He wished he were wearing a short-sleeved shirt.

In a slightly louder voice, Val asked, "New girl friend?"

Ben's tone went in the opposite direction. "You know better than that."

She withdrew her hand. "Anyway, it's divine to see you. Get whatever you need, and we'll chat again later." With a gesture in the form of a sway, she went off, to be claimed immediately by a nearby couple.

Ben continued to stand facing the table. A tremor had his face alive. He blinked frequently. When he brought the glass to his mouth it tapped against his teeth.

Putting the drink down again, untasted, Ben turned and went out to the hallway. He walked back past the staircase and under it into the guest lavatory. He locked the door. What he had meant to do was work at getting control of his emotions. Instead, they rose to an implacable pitch. With a gasp he shot up both hands to cover his face and into them mumbled, "Val, oh, Val."

Ben had fallen in love with his superior's wife after having disliked her for eight years. It was not a virulent dislike. Val Farnsworth he could take or leave. He thought her empty and artificial.

She had been married for some time when they first met, when Harry Farnsworth came in to head Domestic. He, a prize captured from another bank, soon became Ben's friend and mentor. There was a lot of off-duty socialising. Ben sometimes weekended at the cottage, he put the Farnsworths up if they'd had a late night on the town. Harry and Ben several times took girls with them on business trips to the north. Ben liked Harry and tolerated his wife.

One autumn Sunday, the three were having tea by the living room fire. The Farnsworths were in jeans and ragged sweaters. They liked to play bohemian at weekends. Also, Harry did most of the cooking then, while Val worked at her hobby, painting.

This afternoon, running a hand over her short brown hair from back to front, Val said, "Ben, I've decided to give in."

"Great. I can't tell you how pleased I am. What are you talking about?"

Harry chuckled, slopping his tea. "I ask her that ten times a day."

"Don't start getting at me, you two," Val said. "I mean my work. You're always asking to see it, Ben."

He could recall no occasion when he had made such a request. Nodding, he filled his mouth with watercress sandwich.

Val, "Okay. So today I give in."

Harry said an earnest, "She's coming along splendidly, splendidly. Aren't you, old girl?"

"I think so," his wife said with the intensity of an amateur. "I think I'm really getting there."

Ben swallowed his food. "Fine. Let's go."

Val took him upstairs, leaving her husband to his chores in the kitchen. The studio, at the rear of the house, was a new extension that had on the lower level a study for Harry. Its exterior was in reproduction keeping with the Georgian whole.

Although Ben didn't know it, then or ever, it was the paintings that started him falling in love with Val. They were terrible. He had seen better daubs by school children.

As he stood in the middle of the room and looked around, Ben experienced a curious emotion. To him it was fairly alien, except when projected inwards. The feeling was pity.

Val had stayed by the door. She asked, "Well?" Her tone had a taut quality.

Ben turned to look at her. Her arms were tightly folded. She seemed to have grown smaller. He said, nodding, "They're good, Val. Listen. They're very good, indeed."

She watched him steadily. "Ben, do you mean that?"

"Of course I do. Absolutely."

"Harry says—he told me a few days ago—he says you know quite a bit about painting."

Ben reduced the exaggeration without giving it its proper

death. "I know a little, yes. I've taken some canvases as collateral. We've dozens in the vaults."

Val unfolded her arms and clasped her hands behind. "Please tell me what my things are really like."

Before Ben could begin to answer, Val said, turning her head to the side, "Harry's calling. Damn. I knew he'd get stuck with the marinade. Back in a sec."

Alone, Ben looked around again at the streaky canvases. He was struggling hard to remember bits of art expertise he had heard and read. Odd words came to him—cohesion, plasticity, verve.

That drained as the pity came back. He saw loneliness, a craving for understanding, a need to be seen as someone special. He saw a loner, one against the philistine world. He saw himself.

On Val's return, Ben talked a lot of fine-sounding phrases, at the same time wondering how he could have been so wrong about Val Farnsworth all these years. She was not shallow at all. And her artificiality, that was there, but it was the social cover to hide her depth.

The pink tingle that his flattery brought to Val's cheeks gave Ben a pleasure that surprised him with its strength.

For the next two weeks, using her art as his excuse, Ben telephoned Val and saw her on every possible occasion. He listened to her, watched her. By the end of that fortnight, his emotional conversion was complete. Ben had extended the love of himself to a female mirror.

One afternoon, leaving the cottage, instead of giving Val the usual peck on the cheek, he pulled her into his arms and kissed her full on the mouth. He hadn't meant to do it. He was as surprised as Val seemed to be when, hands to his chest, she pushed herself back. They stared at each other.

"Ben," she said. "No."

He began to fumble out words, explain his love. It was

messy, a jumble. He was stricken. And all the time Val was shaking her head and easing him out of the house.

He found himself looking at the closed door. Dazed, he got in his car and drove away.

Later that day, he was more coherent when he telephoned. Val heard him out and then said, gently, "No, Ben. That's final. I don't want to hear another word about it."

But she did. For two months Ben pressed his campaign. Phone calls followed love letters which followed visits to the cottage. He learned from Harry when Val would be in town and contrived a meeting. He sent gifts, whose prompt return never stopped him from sending more.

Val was understanding. At no time did she act curt. Her smile was regretful. When they were at the cottage she wouldn't thrust him away but eel herself from his attempted embraces.

Ben became convinced that she was in love with him. He could accept no other conclusion. He had always believed in justice for himself.

But there seemed to be no hope that he could make her break her marriage vows. And on a meeting in town, she told him with unintended cruelty, putting his love down to a petty level, "Ben, what you need is a hobby."

On Friday night Jill drove home quickly from work. Going by the Royal Coach, she looked at it with affection. She stopped to buy an apple pie and a loaf of country-style bread, a cooked chicken and a small carton of paté.

At the house she hurried inside and up to her flat. The following hour was frantic. Jill tidied, made the bathroom as impersonal as possible, put the chicken in the oven on a low light and prepared vegetables. She showered, changed into a crimson trouser suit, brushed her hair one hundred and fifty times. She put on make-up with slow care, ignoring urgency. She opened out the dining table in the main room, set it, arranged tangerines around the candles, formed the napkins into mitres. She checked three times that the white wine was chilling. She put the couch cushions back where they had been before she had changed them.

At five minutes to seven, when Ben was due, Jill thought of twenty things still undone. In a panic, running from one half-finished job to another, she polished her shoes and stacked discs on the record player, set a vase of paper flowers in the dead hearth and touched perfume on her wrists, changed the cushions again and put on ear-rings, took down the poster of her favourite movie he-man and lay on the coffee table a book of poetry. She put on more make-up.

At five minutes after seven, Jill knew, beyond a shadow of a doubt, that Ben wasn't going to show. Which she forgot immediately as there came a knock on the door. She strolled there, chin up.

Ben was handsome in a blazer and a scarf held with a ring. He had brought a single rose. Jill enthused about it as she drew him in and ushered him onto the couch with the coffee table. She put the flower between the candles before going out for gin and tonics.

From the kitchen she called, "Put the record player on if you like, Ben."

"Right," he said.

Jill felt warm at having a man do things for her. She smiled while slicing the lemon.

Half an hour later, when Jill was swirling peel around the bottom of her near-empty glass, it occurred to her, mildly, that she should show Ben the rifle. She was taken unawares. The talk had been about a new play. The thought came again.

Show him the gun.

Jill was glad at least that she hadn't absentmindedly spoken the frail idea aloud. She ignored it, however. She was playing silly, risky games with herself.

Show him the gun. Do it now.

Jill asked, "How's your drink? Like another before dinner?"

Ben waggled his glass. "I'm fine. But the *Sunday Times* said it was all a matter of miscasting."

Jill said, "Show him . . ."

Ben raised his eyebrows. "What was that?"

"A good show," Jill fumbled, getting up quickly to hide her face. "Entertaining." She moved away. "I'll check on the veges."

"If it's allowed, I'll look through your records."

"Go ahead."

Jill went into the kitchen. She was hot and flustered. She made herself busy checking pans, slicing bread for the toaster and dividing the paté into two portions. She straightened.

Show the rifle. Do it at once. He will understand. Showing him is sensible.

Unlike before, in the other room, the thoughts now were strong. It seemed that she was firmly set on this wild idea. So maybe it wasn't so wild. Maybe it did make sense. But still.

Jill had wandered over to the doorway, was looking into the main room at Ben, who knelt by the stack of records. He was absorbed, elbow on knee, hand to the side of his head.

Show him the rifle.

Jill said a fast, "Ben?"

"Mmm?"

"Do you know anything about guns?"

"A bit," he answered absently, not turning around.

"Well, listen. Listen. I'd like to show you one."

"Fine," he said, turning as he rose. "Wheel it out."

With a feeling of release, Jill retreated, left the kitchen by another doorway, went along a passage to her bedroom. She got the rifle from the wardrobe and took it back to where Ben stood by the couch.

He asked, jocular, "Where d'you keep this thing, under the bath?"

"In my wardrobe."

He took the gun from her. "It's a beauty. Is it yours?"

Jill paused, as if she expected help from somewhere. None came. She said, "Well, it's like this."

Ben sat down and put the rifle on the coffee table. Jill picked up the book of poetry and went toward the shelves. "My father," she went on. "The last time they were down here. He bought it. Loads cheaper than up in Wales, he said. At the last minute they flew back instead of going by train. So he left it here until another time."

"I see."

Jill smiled. "What kind is it—a forty-five?"

Ben laughed. "That's a hand-gun, a baby cannon. This, young lady, is a three-o-three."

"He's going to use it for rabbits."

"Just the thing," Ben said. "But if he hasn't got a licence for it yet, you might get into trouble."

"Oh?"

"I shouldn't mention it to anyone else, if if I were you."

"I won't. Let me put it back. Dangerous thing."

"Can't hurt anyone. It's not loaded. Shall I put it back for you?"

"Please. Just through there."

Dinner was a success. Since Jill had never had a flop of a meal, she didn't know why she always worried beforehand. They had paté with toast, chicken with boiled potatoes and asparagus tips, apple pie with cheese. They got through a bottle and a half of wine. Ben was complimentary about everything, which Jill accepted as honest, though she herself felt sure the asparagus had given away its canned origins.

They went back to the couch with their coffee. Ben declined a liqueur. After a minute's idle talk on pop music, he said, "Excuse me." He got up and left the room.

Jill assumed that he was going to the bathroom, but she heard the flat door open and close. She shrugged, sipped coffee, concluded that he had gone to get something from the car. She perked on thinking: A present?

Five minutes passed.

Ten minutes passed.

Twenty minutes passed.

Jill stayed on the couch, growing more bewildered with every second that went by. She expected the door to open again at any moment; and when it finally did she started with nerves.

Ben came in. He said, "It was something about the Stones. I'll check the sleeve."

More bewildered, even concerned, Jill watched him go over to the stack of records on the low shelf, kneel down as before and rest his head on a hand as he sorted through the discs.

You imagined it. Silly thing. You thought he had gone out and was away nearly half an hour. He went to the bathroom. He was gone only a few minutes.

That isn't possible, Jill thought. I couldn't have fancied the whole thing. It was too . . .

You imagined it. You were day-dreaming. You were mistaken about hearing the door. It was the door of the bathroom. Why on earth would he go outside? Ask him.

Jill leaned forward, but then changed her mind. It had, of course, been imagination. The wine. She had fallen into a doze or a reverie. Of course he hadn't gone out.

She asked, "Ben, did I hear you open the front door a few minutes ago?"

He shook his head. "No."

"I thought not. It was Miss Kelly upstairs."

Yes, she mused, it was. Certainly. She should have thought of that before. It had to be the answer. If Ben hadn't gone out, and if she hadn't imagined his long absence, then that meant . . .

But Jill left it there. She got up and asked brightly, "Who's for more coffee?"

On Monday morning Ben left Highgate Village at nine. He was dressed for business. He hummed cheerfully. The long walk he had taken with Jill Parr yesterday afternoon had ensured a deep sleep without recourse to the usual pills. His pills, in any case, had been used much less these last few weeks.

It was nine-thirty when Ben, heading east, parked the Jaguar in a busy commercial district. He got out, took off his suit coat and left it on the seat, not an unusual act on a warm morning. He locked the car and began to walk. The store was at the far end of the shopping area.

As he walked, glancing in windows, Ben rolled up his shirt sleeves. It made him think of Val. But there were few things that didn't invoke her form or face or voice. Ben had found it easier to dismiss Val from his mind on these occasions and dwell instead on her husband.

Sleeves up, Ben pulled a silk scarf from his hip pocket. He looped it around his neck and knotted it so that his collar and tie were hidden. There was no need for him to check if this were so; he had practiced at home. But, telling himself better safe than sorry, he stopped to look in a window so he could get a careful sighting on his reflection.

Walking on, he took from the breast pocket of his shirt a pair of sunglasses. He put them on. They were the heavy type with finger-thick frames and dark glass.

As with the jacket and the sleeves, his glasses were apt in this weather, Ben told himself. Only the scarf was odd. Not that it made any difference. It was just good that he was aware of the oddness, was on to every detail and nuance.

He came to the sporting goods store. Inside as he entered, a char was mopping the floor, a delivery man was drumming his fingers on the invoice he wanted signed, two schoolboys argued at a stack of fishing rods, a man in a warehouse coat asked the char to please hurry it up. It was the early confusion Ben had hoped for.

He went to the counter's far end. From behind it, a youth rose. He asked, "Something?"

Ben said, "I want a box of point twenty-two shells, please."

The boy blinked stupidly. "You want what, mate?"

Ben had a fleeting panic. He smiled and said, "Bullets for a rifle. It's a twenty-two."

"A box of two-twos, you want."

"That's right."

The youth chanted, "Fifty, hundred, two hundred, five."

"What?" The panic again.

"What size box you want?"

"The fifty, please. One box."

"Make?"

"Any."

The youth put a dirty finger in one nostril. "Some's cheaper than others. Which d'you usually get?"

"I don't. It's a present. Give me the best."

One minute later Ben was back on the street and heading for his car. He felt annoyed with himself for those small panics. It wasn't his fault if he happened to get served by a clod.

Ben took off his scarf and wrapped it around the small box of ammunition. He admitted that the panic was because the purchase was something he had been dreading. It was a strong link. But unavoidable. Since in none of the dozen stores and sports departments he had been in had shells been on display, but always stored in drawers or under the counter, there was no way he could think of to get Jill to pick up a box.

In any event, he felt that that would be pushing the girl too far. As it was, he was making her go very close to the edge. She could crack. It was, yes, a weakness in the plan. As was the chance of her taking fright and getting rid of the gun.

In which case, Ben thought, refusing to be pulled down, in which case he would start all over again and make her get another. And what a bright idea that had been on Friday, telling her the rifle was a .303. Later, she would be much less likely to make a connexion.

His sleeves were down and his sunglasses off by the time he reached the car. He unlocked it, put on his jacket and got in. The silk-wrapped box he put under the seat, after giving it a farewell squeeze. He felt excited. Soon, he promised. A week or two. No more. After that, get slowly organised. Lots to be done. For one, get rid of that boat.

Ben had bought the luxury toy within a week of Val saying that he needed a hobby. One was connected with the other only in a roundabout way. Ben had been impressed by reading, in a press account of an inquest on a Thames death, the coroner's condemnation of inefficient weekend sailing. People needed licences to drive cars, he said, but any idiot was allowed to operate a boat; it was a rare weekend on the river that didn't see at least one death.

That seemed to be the answer.

On the scales held by Ben's personal blind goddess, as his love for Val rose at one side, his feelings for Harry sank at the other. The feelings did not become hate. Harry turned into a nonentity, a thing, a nuisance, an object such as, for instance, a barrier.

Being convinced of Val's love, Ben knew she would gladly belong to him once her womanising husband ceased to exist. Ben had no trouble deciding to kill Harry.

The how of the matter, though, that soon became apparent as a real problem. Killing was one thing, staying blameless quite another. The boating accident idea Ben soon called off. What at first had seemed so obviously simple, developed into a monster of a hundred detailed heads. It also had one extremely large head. That was that Ben would have to be there, on the scene. There was no way for him to disassociate himself from the accident. So, there was not only the danger of Val suspecting, but also the police.

Weeks passed. Ben chose and discarded a score of killing methods. He scoured newspapers and became an avid reader of murder fiction. Val he saw as little as he was able without making her or Harry curious; he was afraid he would be tempted into rushing into a risky extermination.

The solution came at last, as he had known all along it would. He had not really been worried in the slightest. A book on hypnotism gave him the idea—after he had remembered Jill Parr.

It was a little after ten when Ben went into the bank. Humming, he ascended the staircase and strode along the gallery. The door next to his own was open. Passing it, he glanced in. Harry Farnsworth saw him and called, "Ben. Here a minute."

Ben went in. He smiled. He felt almost benevolent toward his superior. "Hello, Harry. Nice weekend?"

"Yes. The usual. You?"

"Pleasant. By the way, thanks again for the Thursday bash."

"You didn't stay long."

"Harry, the older I get the more careful I am about driving if I've had a few drinks."

Farnsworth nodded, with reluctance it seemed. "I suppose. Yes, that's wise." He got up from behind his desk, flapping a hand at the cigarette ash on his waistcoat. "I'm a bit browned off this A.M., as a matter of fact."

"Why's that? Some dolly let you down?"

Harry gave another flap with his hand. "Business. Just heard I've a board of governors' dinner tomorrow night."

Ben had been casually looking out of the window. He swung around fast. "What?"

Farnsworth looked taken aback. "I said I had a top-dog dinner on tomorrow night."

"But I thought that was going to be later."

"So did I. Bloody pain in the neck. You simply have no idea how incredibly boring these deals are."

Ben was settling, had himself under control. He said, "I can imagine."

Harry Farnsworth squared his shoulders. "Still, I know the ropes. I have it worked out to the minute. I've been through hundreds of these bloody things."

"Poor Harry."

"Anyway, look at these papers for me, will you. There's your okay on here and it seems to me . . ."

It was fifteen minutes before Ben could get away. He went into his office, sat at the desk and leaned back, hands interlocked on his chest. He had to decide now. If he didn't do it tomorrow night, he might have to wait weeks. Which was it to be, Tuesday or sometime?

Later that day, Jill heard her telephone ringing as she went upstairs. She hurried, let herself in the flat and ran to grab up the receiver. "Hello?"

"Hi, Jill. Ben here. I've called you twice already."

"I just got in, Ben. This very minute." She thought he sounded slightly peeved.

"Okay. Now look. About tomorrow night. Are you doing anything?"

Jill smiled. "No. I'm as free as the air."

"That's good. I'd like to come around and see you, at about nine-thirty, if that'd be all right."

"Perfect, Ben, of course."

He said, "There's a matter I'd like to discuss with you. I'd want to be sure we wouldn't be interrupted. So if you think a neighbour or friend might drop in unexpectedly, I'd rather you said so now."

"You sound very mysterious."

There was a pause. "Well, I don't mean to," Ben said. "It's simply that this matter is rather important. I'd be annoyed if we had even one interruption."

"Ben, no one ever calls here unexpectedly. Well, hardly ever."

"So there is a possibility." His tone was heavy, like a tired good-bye. "I see."

"Tell you what," Jill said. "I'll drop a hint to the neighbours and call any friends who might get the unlikely idea of stopping by."

His voice became brighter. "Good. Good girl. That should do it."

Jill said, "But you must tell me what it's all about. I'll die of curiosity before tomorrow night."

"No you won't," Ben said lightly. "And it's nothing sensational. Until tomorrow at nine-thirty, then. 'Bye for now."

Heading for the kitchen, Jill didn't know whether to be up or down. It was good that she would be seeing Ben on Tuesday, but bad that she had no notion of what to expect. Like most women, Jill loved surprises as long as she knew about them beforehand.

Through dinner and the rest of the evening, Jill returned to the question of what Ben wanted to see her about so particularly. She came up with several reasons: He was going to offer her a job; he wanted to discuss a joint vacation; he needed information on Almanacum Imports Ltd.; he would tell her that he had quit his job and was leaving the country; he would confess about his wife and children; he wanted her to know that he had a terminal disease.

After that last one, Jill stopped looking. One other idea came of its own accord while she was getting ready for bed. She thought: He's going to propose. Blushing, Jill became furiously busy laying out clean clothes.

Next day, at the mid-morning coffee break, Jill telephoned the only person she knew who might even remotely be inclined to call in at the flat unannounced. She explained the situation. May Wilson said:

"Don't worry. I've got a summer cold. I wouldn't leave the house for God. My nose is like a tomato."

"But look. What d'you think he wants?"

"You mean you don't know? Come on, Jillian Parr. You're not that innocent."

"What?"

"My dear girl, the man's going to seduce you. Or try to."

"Nonsense," Jill said, her voice a creak. "Ben's not the type for that."

"If he's male, he's the type."

"Must go now," Jill said with more coolness than she had intended. "Call you soon."

Later, she thought about May's forecast. She didn't believe it. Ben seemed low on passion. At least, so far in the relationship. Their love-making was always sedate. On Friday, after dinner, when they had necked for a while on the couch, he had been even more restrained than usual. Ben, assuredly, was the cerebral kind.

Later still, Jill asked Mr. Olivieri if he had heard of Waringford and Myer. Her boss said he had, vaguely, it was a bank or insurance company. So that ruled out Almanacum Imports Ltd. looking for a loan. Jill decided to give it up, once and for all and completely. Within ten minutes she was wondering if Ben wanted to talk about . . .

After work she drove home in a roundabout way to pass time. At the house she saw Mrs. Parkinson looking through her window. They both waved. Jill went over to the window instead of to the door. Her beak-faced neighbour shot up the window and they exchanged pleasantries.

Jill, pretending that she wasn't remembering May Wilson's prophecy, decided on a simple put-off that could not be construed in any manner other than that stated.

She said, "I've had an exhausting day. I'm going straight to bed after I've had a snack."

Mrs. Parkinson was sympathetic. She recommended earplugs as a guard against these here young louts as what was always racing around the streets on their motor bikes.

They parted and Jill went inside. Miss Kelly would not have to be warded off; she had never come down to visit yet, and in any case was always in bed by nine.

Jill had a leisurely shower, was particular about the underclothes she chose, used more scent than normal, put on a short jersey skirt and a skinny sweater with a low neckline. As this was an at-home deal more than a date, she kept cosmetics to the minimum and brushed her hair in a way that made it look as if it hadn't been brushed all day.

Following a sandwich supper, Jill tried to read. It was impossible. She began to pace. The thud of her feet, which would be heard below, reminded her that she was supposed to be in bed. And that, as she sat, made her wonder if Mrs. Parkinson, catching sight of Ben, might get protective and tell him not to disturb the tired working girl.

At nine-fifteen Jill went softly downstairs. Still careful about noise she drew the house door open. She stood there within the frame, one foot tapping, watching the cars go by. It was dusk

now. Mrs. Parkinson's curtains were drawn. Jill waited anyway.

It was exactly nine-thirty when Ben appeared. He smiled
and blew a kiss, yet Jill thought he had a faint look of strain,
especially around the eyes. As he came through the gateway
she saw that he carried a roll of canvas a yard long.

A painting? she mused. He's going to give me a picture?
That was possible because on Sunday, during their walk, she,
for some unknown reason, had kept on and on about painting.

While thinking thus, Jill had greeted Ben, brought him inside and led the way upstairs. They went into the main room
and sat on the couch.

Jill said, "I didn't see your Jag go by."

"I came from the other direction," Ben said. "Will you excuse me for a minute?"

"Why, yes."

He got up again from his rest of a few seconds. Still holding
the canvas he left the room.

Jill leaned forward. She was listening acutely. She heard
sounds from along the passage; next, returning footsteps; next,
the flat door opening and closing. The rest was silence.

Jill leaned back. She drew her legs up onto the seat, doubled them to her closely. Her arms she crossed over her
breasts. She stared vacantly into space. After a moment, she
began to tremble.

Smooth, Ben assured himself as he strode to the car. Everything is as smooth as oil. It had been a queasy moment, yes,
seeing the dumb bitch in the doorway, and thinking she was
going to say their talk was off, she had to go out. But the girl
was just keen, that's all. Smitten. She would stay there safe and
quiet for the hour.

Ben unlocked his Jaguar. He was pleased with himself for
not having left it unlocked, even though he had known he

would be gone mere minutes. Someone could have jumped in and crossed the wires. So--you had to watch the details. Then the big things took care of themselves. Like pennies and pounds.

After putting the canvas-wrapped rifle behind the front seat, Ben looked all around. While doing so, he tugged into tighter fit the gloves he had put on before taking the gun out of the wardrobe.

In his scrutiny around the street he left out no window or doorway. It was almost fully dark now. But he saw safety, the same lack of observers as when he had stopped.

He got in, started the motor, drove off. He went swiftly. Time was an important factor. All would go well if there were none of those unforeseens that you couldn't do anything about --a flat tyre, a traffic jam, perhaps an accident, being stopped by the police for speeding.

But that would simply mean cancellation for tonight. The show would go on another time. If any of those things happened on the way back--that was a different matter.

Ben shook his head. It was a quick, nervous action, almost like a series of twitches. There were white marks of pucker around his mouth.

No, he thought. The first two didn't matter. The others, they could be avoided by cautious driving. They would have been rendered irrelevant with a hired car and the excuse of having left all papers behind. But still.

Ben had learned that it was impossible to rent a car without a driver's licence and other identification. Some firms, scorning cash, would let their cars out only on presentation of a credit card. Forgery, stealing someone else's papers—these Ben had dismissed as dangerous complications. Stealing a car had also been rejected. If its loss were discovered at once, if the police were on the lookout for it . . .

Ben, speeding along a deserted residential street, drew in

deep breaths through his nose. He could feel it getting to work now, the tranquiliser he had taken just before leaving High-gate Village. Smooth, he told himself.

He looked at his wristwatch and then at the clock in the dashboard. Both had been synchronised from the radio time signal. They were dead right, and if one should somehow fail, he still had the other. He needed to get there before ten.

Harry Farnsworth, Ben knew, would be timing his business dinner accurately. He would get away by nine-thirty at the latest—though his driving would be fairly steady because of the wine he had drunk out of boredom. He would want to be home by ten-fifteen to watch his favourite television pro-gramme, a nightly round-up of sporting events. Only a real night out or a new flirtation could make him miss that one.

Harry would pass the junction between ten o'clock and ten minutes past. It had happened that way twice in the past month. Ben had been there to see.

Traffic lights loomed ahead. Ben put on speed to reach them while the green was still showing. He made it and went into a screeching right turn.

He was on a main thruway now. He lowered his foot on the accelerator. His eyes were keen on the well-lighted distance in front and the mirror's picture of the rear. He was unlikely to be taken unawares by a patrol car and he felt sure that there were no radar traps on this section.

Ben's mouth took on a different kind of tension. The puckers went. The bottom lip came forward as his jaw re-sponded to his determination and eagerness for speed. He thought he was doing remarkably well, and that he had never doubted such would be the case.

Alibi, he mused. That had been the big stumbling block. Miss Parr had given him the solution, as well as conveniently easing matters in acquiring a weapon. All he need do when he got back there, after an absence of perhaps one and a quarter hours, no more, was to make her believe that said absence had been imagined. And, to render his presence more memorable, a red-letter night she was unlikely to forget, he would suggest that they get engaged. She might decline, of course. But the occasion would be remembered.

Ben smiled at the idea of the little secretary declining to become engaged to him. And some people thought he had no sense of humour.

The thruway ended. Ben turned back into residential streets again. They were as good as empty of moving traffic, and would stay that way until the pubs closed, by which time he would be safely back at Cheever Street—after a brief stop on the way to get rid of the gun. A field would do. Perhaps a river. It didn't matter.

Ben patted his jacket pocket to feel the nine bullets. The other forty-one he had dropped into the Thames late yesterday, from Westminster Bridge, while leaning there looking at a sunset. The carton had been ripped up and flushed down the toilet.

Ben began to hum. He stopped that on telling himself he must avoid over-confidence. Sober care, that was the watchword.

Ben also stopped himself when he began to think about Val. He was used to that now. He had many substitutes as well as Harry that gave him a feeling of connexion without disturbing his emotions. He could think of Georgian cottages, or short-hair styles, or an art-supply shop, or paintings.

Ben thought about that canvas around the gun. It was a piece of old sailcloth. Since it couldn't be traced to him, instead of taking it back home as planned he would throw it away. Why? Because the rifle might leave a trace of itself on the material, a spot of oil, even a smell. Police technology was pretty smart nowadays. But then, Ben thought, so am I.

He checked both timepieces. It lacked eleven minutes of ten

o'clock and he was within five minutes of the junction.
Smooth.

He had left houses behind now. He was on a winding country road. Soon he turned off onto a road that was narrower,
then again onto a lane. His lights cut through the darkness.

He rounded a final bend. There ahead, glowing feebly with
its inside light, was the telephone booth on the point of the
fork.

Ben slowed. He reached the junction, angled to its right,
crawled on for another ten yards and then stopped. He put the
shift into reverse, twisted around in his seat and carefully
backed off the unfenced road. The ground hard here—he had
checked—there would be no tyre marks.

When he halted the Jaguar it was between trees and the
high bushes behind the telephone booth; virtually hidden. He
switched off motor and lights.

Ben opened the door. He got out and stood listening. All he
could hear was bird-rustle in the trees, plus ticks and whines
from his car as it settled to rest.

Although the night was moonless, there were stars by their
seeable thousands. They gave sufficient illumination when
aided by a glimmer from the telephone booth.

Ben looked at his watch. It told him three minutes to ten.
He leaned inside the car and brought out the canvas roll, let
the gun slide out butt first to the ground, threw the canvas
back inside.

A high-pitched sound made him stiffen. He next recognised
the noise as that of an approaching car. But it was not from
the direction he was concerned with. Even so, Ben frowned.
He was counting on the sparsity of traffic associated with this
area—apart from the morning departure and evening return of
commuters.

The sound grew, headlights appeared flickingly through the
trees. The car was coming along the left-hand fork. Ben

watched the approach and unconsciously sank into a crouch.

The car went by. Roar and tear of brightness gone, all was back to the dim silence. Ben opened the rifle's magazine. He fed it with bullets, bringing them one at a time from his pocket. He closed the magazine again.

Leaving the car he moved to a place near the edge of the bushes. From here he had a clear view of the lane beyond the telephone box, the way Harry Farnsworth would come.

The luminous dial of Ben's watch told him one minute to ten. He hoped Harry wouldn't be late. Not that it really mattered, not in terms of accomplishment. But the less time spent away from Cheever Street the better.

Ben felt calm. Not nervous, not over-confident. Calm. The rest was going to be child's play.

After shooting Harry Farnsworth, Ben would take his keys, and leave. Just that. Harry's car, his watch and ring, his cash, they would not be touched. The police would reach an obvious conclusion: The executive of Waringford and Myer had been killed by a gang who thought they could get into the bank and its vaults with the key-ring.

It was a nice touch, Ben had thought. He still thought so. Its gist value lay in the fact that the police would not go nosing around for motives. They would have one. A motive too subtle to be suspect—it was not going to jump out at them straight away; hours or days might pass before anyone realised that the dead man's keys were missing.

That they were all for personal effects, would not even open the bank's back gate, would have no bearing. There were more gangs of ill-informed bunglers than those led by the master criminals of fiction.

And naturally, Ben mused, no one was going to murmur if Harry Farnsworth's best friend paid constant attention to the widow. That was normal procedure. It was also fairly common for widow and friend to form a romantic attachment born of a shared mourning—after a decent time span, say three or four months.

Ben was smiling as he checked his watch again. One minute past ten. It wouldn't be long now. And maybe that was the car.

The sound, growing, came from the right direction. Looking that way through the leaves, Ben could see headlights streaking the sky. The car was not going fast. It was a good prospect.

The twin beams came into view. Ben tutted. He could tell by the shape of the lights' cowling, even before the car body became clear, that this was not the Farnsworth Rover. He eased back from the edge of the bushes.

The car was slowing. Ben went into that crouch again. He increased it greatly, nearly squatting, when the car came to a stop in front of the telephone booth.

No, Ben thought. This rotten luck couldn't happen to me.

There were two women in the car, a new Renault. This Ben saw as the driver brought the dome light alive by opening her door. The women were middle-aged and had blue hair. They were ten feet from where Ben crouched. He was clinging to hope because the car's motor had been left ticking over.

The driver said, "I'm sure I gave you the number."

The passenger said, "Darling, I keep telling you that you didn't. I keep telling you."

"You know how forgetful you are, darling." She was searching the pockets of her dress and cardigan. "I'm positive I haven't got it."

"And so am I. We'll have to go back."

Go, Ben was urging. He thought there was still hope if the two old crows left at once. His watch said three minutes past.

The driver asked, "You've looked in all your pockets, darling?"

"I keep telling you. Let's go back."

"Honestly," the driver fumed, getting back into her seat. "Honestly." She slammed the door, grated gears. The car moved off and went back the way it had come.

Ben stood upright. He wondered if the women meant to return to the telephone box, and if so, how long would that take. He also questioned what he would do if a car happened to pass at the moment he was dealing with Harry Farnsworth. The simple task had now taken on the hue of a complex project.

Ben's confidence told him he should not let himself be rattled by a couple of old bitches who didn't know what they were doing. They were probably lost anyway and might never find their way back here. And as for another—

A flash of light hit the sky where Ben had his eyes fixed. He moved quickly back to the edge of the bushes. The brightness swung and lurched as its source wound the lane. The lights splattered into view. Ben strained forward.

Yes, the car was a Rover.

Although Ben knew it was possible for a Rover to appear at this spot at this time and not be the Farnsworth car, he ignored that as an absurd coincidence.

He lay the rifle down on the ground. Straightening, he ran his hands over himself in an absent check for neatness. The headlights were blaring, the car was almost here.

Ben stepped clear of cover. At once he was in the brightness. He faced it and began to wave both arms in a halt signal. He heard the Rover's motor lessen. Beyond the glare he could faintly make out an upper shape he knew: Harry Farnsworth.

The car came level. Still slowing, it passed and went on another thirty feet before coming to a gentle stop. Ben moved back to where he had left the rifle.

The car door opened. Farnsworth leaned his upper body out and looked back. He called, "What the hell're you doing here, Ben?" His tone was a mingling of surprise and amusement.

"Harry," Ben said. He lifted the gun from the ground.

"What?" Farnsworth called. He peered, moving his head. "Where are you, Ben? What's wrong?"

Ben spoke the other man's name again, but no louder than before. He wanted to draw him out of the car. He was holding the rifle in both hands, ready to lift it to his shoulder as soon as he had a good, large target. The distance was perfect. Just like the shooting gallery in Leicester Square.

Harry Farnsworth was still moving his head from side to side, as if watching boxers. He called, "I can't see you. What's up, for God's sake?"

"I'm over here."

Harry eased himself out of the car. He stood with one hand on top of the door. From the waist up he was clearly silhouetted against the splash of headlights.

Ben brought the rifle to his shoulder. He aimed. His finger stroked the trigger—and his legs began to shake.

"Ben?" Harry called.

His finger was on the trigger, the aim was right, but Ben was unable to shoot. In amazement he felt the tremor of his legs work its way swiftly upward.

Harry Farnsworth called, "What is it?"

Ben couldn't speak now to answer, loud or soft. His whole body was shaking. His arms drooped.

Suddenly Farnsworth came striding forward. "What the hell is going on here?"

Now, Ben thought. Shoot. You can't miss.

He let the rifle fall to the ground. To stop Farnsworth from seeing it he went forward. His walk was unsteady. He was still astounded.

"Oh, there you are," Harry said.

They stopped with a yard of space between. Harry's face gave away that he didn't know whether to be annoyed or anxious. Ben simply stood there.

Farnsworth stated, "You look upset."

Ben managed, "No. I'm fine."

"Where's your car?"

"Back there."

"Trouble? Accident?"

"No. I'm fine."

Farnsworth put his hands on his hips. "Well, what is it, Ben? Why did you wave me down?"

"A mistake," Ben mumbled. "I thought it was . . . I thought it was another car."

"Oh?"

"Didn't know it was you, Harry. I'm sorry."

Farnsworth showed his hands in a placating gesture. "No sweat, old son. Nothing to be upset about." He paused, then startled Ben with a laugh. "Oh, I see, I see."

"Eh?"

Harry was nodding happily. "Had a date with some filly, did we? Some young thing whose hubby would rather read, eh? It's no wonder we're shaking like a leaf, is it?"

"Well, I—"

"You sly dog, you. And I think I know the very piece."

Ben made the motion of looking at his watch. He didn't know why. He had no interest in the time; in anything. But the move ended this duologue which he was finding a great effort to sustain.

Farnsworth began backing off, hands pushing to stay a protest. "Okay, okay, don't fret. I'm on my way. Wouldn't spoil things for the world. Enjoy yourself, old son." Chuckling, he turned and walked on. He called back, "See you tomorrow."

Now, Ben ordered himself. Get the gun quick.

He stood and watched Harry Farnsworth reach his car, get in, close the door, drive away. He was still there when the taillights had gone and the area was silent again.

TWO

The sun shone out of a languid sky. Those few clouds present, they moved so slowly that they looked to be in danger of falling. At ground level there was no breeze. Insects hummed a complaint at the show-off bird song. It was the kind of English summer day that poets had been lying about for centuries, and which actually did occur.

Trees surrounded the meadow on three sides. The fourth had a stream, now heated to a trickle. Beyond that were more open fields. Blue and yellow flowers spotted the grass like the remains of an Easter egg-hunt.

Near the stream stood a dilapidated wooden building. Its side bore barely discernible lettering that said the hut had once belonged to a football club.

Jill Parr was looking at the hut from the meadow's far end. She thought it sad, the death of somebody's dream. She felt safe in this thought because she herself was so happy.

Wearing shorts and a T-shirt, Jill sat cross-legged on an outspread blanket. In its centre were all the sundries of a picnic, not excluding ants. Mess and liquefied butter showed that the first assault was over.

Jill looked away from the hut at a sound. It, a whimper of comfort, had come from Ben. He lay nearby on the blanket, supine, hands at the back of his head, eyes lazing across the sky.

Jill asked, "Full?"

"Mmm," he said. "Bursting."

"There's more apple pie."

"Oh, God."

Jill smiled. "I'm so happy that I don't mind confessing I didn't make it myself."

He looked at her from the corners of his eyes. "That's the nicest thing you've ever said to me, Jill. Thanks."

She wrinkled her nose. "Race you to that hut and back."

"Go away."

Laughing, Jill got up, uncoiling herself voluptuously and revelling in the freedom of her muscles. She strolled off through the grass, saying, "I'll pick flowers."

Jill felt reborn. Last week, she had sunk from a high to a wretched low. By Saturday night she had been as miserable as at any time in her life. There had been no word from Ben.

Before this Sunday picnic, the last time Jill had seen Ben had been Tuesday. That evening, for some foolish reason, she had built up to three-star quality. She had felt let down when all they did was sit and listen to music. There wasn't even the usual bout of mild necking.

Worse, her imagination had been at work again, and just as she was beginning to think she had finished with all that. She day-dreamed that Ben had gone out. It was incredibly real. But later, watching Ben as he browsed at her bookshelves, she realised that the whole thing had been imagined. She had been upset. Ben too, leaving soon after that, had looked depressed.

Jill's spiritual decline had increased during the following days as Ben failed to telephone. She wondered if she could have said or done something wrong on that odd Tuesday date. She had been on the point of strangling her pride, calling him, when this morning he had rung up to ask, "Like picnics?"

It turned out he'd had to go to Birmingham on business and had not had the opportunity to make contact. All her dreariness and neurotic worrying had been for nothing.

That telephone call had been one of the finest that Jill could remember having. It had lasted about half an hour, unusually long for Ben, who generally kept his calls brief. They had laughed and joked about who would bring what, who would supply this and that, where they would go. After disconnecting, Jill had danced around the room.

She felt like dancing again now, felt like leaping and bounding through the sweet-smelling grass. But Ben might consider her foolish. A glance back showed Jill the all-clear: He was still sky-gazing.

She skipped on, free as a child, her arms poised for balance. When she tripped and went sprawling, she was even more delighted. She rolled and giggled and kicked.

Grinning, Jill got up. She decided while sighing her breathing back to normal to leave the flowers be.

Circling base at a saunter, her eyes on the sprawled figure in technicolour shirt and chinos, Jill mused that he also was happy. That long telephone call was one indication. Another was his smile. He exuded even more confidence and self-satisfaction than when they had started re-dating, if that were possible, and it had to be because it was true. His aura of assurance was strong.

Jill continued circling until Ben sat up. She went over, asking, "Shall we finish the last of that coffee?"

"That's exactly what I was thinking."

"Great minds, and so forth."

He laughed.

Jill emptied the vacuum flask into their plastic cups. Ben toasted her, "To a lovely day with a lovely girl."

"Thank you. And again for the girl."

Ben changed to banter. "When you get to my age, my dear," he said, "you'll know that youth has really flown."

"Poor old soul."

They talked on in the same vein. The joshing gave Jill a feeling of comfort, of permanency. Ben's tease had more force than pretty speeches. His toast had given her the slight, and soon gone, impression that she was being mocked.

Ben emptied his cup and put it down. "Now," he said. "How about that practice?"

"Fine. Let me do a bit of tidying first."

He got up. "I'll be fetching the goods."

While Ben walked off toward the trees, beyond which lay his car, Jill fussed with the crockery and leftovers. She spun the chore out because it made her feel wifely.

Presently she heard voices. Standing, she saw that Ben, on his way back with the rifle, had been stopped by a young couple. But almost as soon as Jill saw this, Ben moved away. The couple went in the other direction.

Ben's attitude had seemed curt, Jill thought, yet she thought it vaguely, for she was having a recurrence of her uneasiness in respect of the rifle. It was a new discomfort, not that of long standing, acquisition.

On Wednesday morning, getting clothes from her wardrobe, Jill had found that the gun was wrapped in canvas. She could not recall having done that, even though she thought about it all through the day. She had put it down to her new absent-mindedness, which was not too satisfying.

It was good, however, Jill mused as she brushed crumbs off the blanket, that since then her mind had acted quite normally. Also, that there seemed to be an explanation for that wrapping.

When Ben had come to collect her for the picnic, he said, "I've got some bullets that might fit that gun of your father's. Let's take it with us and practice shooting."

"Oh, I don't know, Ben. D'you think we should?"

"But of course. It's interesting. We'll roll the gun in a cloth to smuggle it in and out of the house."

"As a matter of fact," Jill said, "I put some canvas around it."

"Smart girl. Perfect."

Obviously, Jill had thought, going to the bedroom, it was with the gun's future transfer in mind that she had wrapped it. But that didn't explain where the material had come from. She knew that she had only imagined seeing Ben with a roll of canvas when he had arrived Tuesday.

Now, Ben stopped by the trees. He waved, calling, "This is the best place." He added, when she went over, "My bullets fit, by the way. Someone left 'em at my place years ago."

"What a coincidence they should be the right size."

"Not really. There are only three sizes."

"Oh, I see," Jill said, dismissingly. "What did that boy and his girl want?"

"Asked if I had a light. I said I didn't smoke. I was short with them, I'm afraid."

"It looked that way, yes."

Ben said, "Foolish of me." He pulled a rueful mouth. "It's just that I was hoping we'd have this place to ourselves. I resented them, I suppose."

Jill touched his arm. She was always impressed by castigation of self. "That's quite understandable, Ben. After all, we did drive a long way to find this spot."

Ben smiled again. "And it's a beauty. An oasis of calm."

"Marvellous."

"But let's get on with our sport. Let me see if I can remember how to handle these things. Haven't shot a rifle since I was fifteen."

Over the following hour, the gun was loaded and emptied many times. Once Ben let Jill put the shells in herself. It was easy. You simply pushed the nine in one behind the other. After that you didn't have to do anything, just keep pulling the trigger—the bullets went into the barrel automatically.

Despite her reservations about the rifle, Jill enjoyed the sport. The learning of it, rather. With Ben's arms around her, his body close, she was not fully concentrating on his many instructions.

Even so, she grasped the rudiments. She was able to hold and aim by herself finally, and once clipped bark off the side of the tree they were aiming at. She liked the smell of gunpowder. It reminded her of fireworks when she was a kid.

The session ended with the appearance, beyond the stream, of a family group—adults, children, dogs. They were making no move to come this way, but Ben said,

"Time we were off anyway. Getting late."

"I suppose so."

"We'll stop at a pub, if you like, have a couple of drinks."

"That sounds lovely, Ben."

Much later, leaving the country pub at twilight, Jill and Ben embraced beside the Jaguar. They kissed. They swayed in time with the piano music coming from the open windows. Jill could have wished for nothing more romantic.

They got in the car and drove away. Jill sat low in the seat with her head resting back. She was content. She knew that Ben felt the same, even without looking at his smile. She could tell by his quiet hum.

"Good afternoon to you, Mr. Armitage."

"And a good afternoon to you, Mr. Jeb."

Ben went up the steps and through the revolving door. He startled a dozen clerks by slapping his leg with the rolled newspaper as he walked to the stairs. In order not to show his amusement he tongued the front of his bottom teeth.

Above on the gallery, Ben became wary as he neared his office. He wanted to avoid Harry Farnsworth. There had been only one meeting since the debacle last Tuesday night. Harry had been raffish and inquisitive, Ben uncomfortable. He could no longer stand the sight of his superior.

Ben passed that door safely, went through his own. He sat

at the desk and opened his newspaper, which he had bought to read at lunch. He found the personal column item he had circled. Followed by a telephone number, it said *Consult Madam Zena, Clairvoyant.*

Ben had seen that single line of type for as many years as he had been in London. It had stuck in his mind because the name was so laughably corny. A vicar's wife might have chosen it as, in disguise, she read a crystal ball at the church fete.

He picked up his telephone and dialled the number. A firm voice said, "Madam Zena speaking."

"Good afternoon, Madam. My name is Williamson. I wonder if I could make an appointment with you for this evening."

"Rather short notice," the woman said. "But as it happens, I have a cancellation. That's at seven o'clock. Would that suit?"

"Perfectly. Thank you."

"I'll give you the address."

After disconnecting, Ben put the scribbled address in his pocket and turned to paperwork. It was some time before his attention was broken. This was by a laugh that filtered through from next door.

Ben squirmed. Once again he was reminded of last week, the junction of country lanes, his failure there, the way he had shaken as if with palsy. Ben saw the scene and relived its aftermath, that second attack of trembling during which he had been shocked to find he wanted to call on his mother for help.

Ben got up, circled the desk, sat again and ran smoothing hands down his tie. In defence he remembered how well he had recovered from the debacle. He had been quite calm back at Cheever Street when, after putting the rifle back in its place, he had set about making Jill believe she had imagined his absence—which part of the scheme was no longer necessary, he knew, but making it succeed had lessened the failure of the other part.

From then until Saturday had been a dreary time for Ben. He had been forced to accept that he was incapable of killing. He was, he told himself, far too sensitive. He simply lacked the vital crudeness. What Ben could not accept was that he would have to forget the whole plan. He could not turn back. He had sold himself to a future with Val. Without her, life was nothing.

But there seemed no answer. All those that did occur to Ben he had to dismiss as impossible, farcical or dangerous, from sending poisoned food through the mail to hiring a professional killer. He spent a bleak few days.

The answer came Saturday afternoon. He was sitting on his balcony. Idly, his eyes had picked out the approximate area where Cheever Street lay, some three miles distant as the crow flies. The answer made him stand; stand and slowly raise his arms at the sides.

It was perfection. Not only would he not be directly involved, he would have no need for a phony alibi. He would have a real one, be spending the evening with friends. The plan, in fact, was vastly superior to the original.

There had been just enough time left before the shops closed for Ben to buy more shells. Dressed as previously, he had gone to the same store. Danger was reduced by limiting the number of people who could make even the slightest connexion between himself and shooting.

Now, recovered from his discomfort brought by Farnsworth's laugh, Ben was able to preen in recognition of his scheme. It was brilliant. His future was assured.

Closing his eyes, Ben allowed himself a rare luxury. He thought about Val.

At four-fifteen he left the bank and drove home, stopping once to pick up spare ribs at a take-away cafe. He ate quickly and without interest. Afterwards he sorted laundry to pass the time.

At last Ben judged that Jill Parr would now be home from work. He sat down. He was stimulated. This was an important test. The distance between here and Cheever Street was roughly the same as that between the Minstrel Boy and the area of the Farnsworth cottage. It was vital to know if his mental power was as efficient from this far as it was close up. Vital, that is, to the alibi. The rest was guaranteed.

Ben put the tips of his fingers to his temples. Concentrating hard, he pictured Jill Parr's face. He saw it in detail, especially the eyes. He looked at them closely while thinking with a pause separating each phrase:

You want to call Ben. It is a good idea. He will be pleased to hear from you. The number is in the book. Give him a ring. No need to be shy.

Ben kept it up for two minutes, eased off, went back to full pressure, though still slowly, spacing to allow digestion.

As he was easing off from the second bout, the telephone shrilled. Grinning, he snatched up the receiver and gave his number. A light female voice said, "Hello, Ben. It's me."

"Jill. What a pleasant surprise."

"Yes, well, I thought I'd call and say thanks again for the picnic yesterday. I had a marvellous time."

"Good. I'm so glad. I did too. That salad of yours . . ."

When Ben rang off five minutes later he had a date to pick Jill up the next night to go for a drive. It was all part of his scheme, which, he now knew—had proved—was going to be an all-round success.

Next, Ben thought, a little more knowledge. But only for the sake of curiosity.

He went downstairs to drive to St. John's Wood.

It was a large, cheaply-built block of flats. A smell of cooking pervaded the stairways. Ben was still not prepared, however, for the prosaic appearance of the woman who called herself Madam Zena.

She opened the door to his knock, stood aside and said, "Come in, young man."

She was past sixty, tall and stout. Immense breasts pushed out swoopingly her print dress and cowed back a cardigan that was covered with darns. The toecaps had worn away on her slippers. Short on brow, the face was broad and plain. Her eyes were mild, pleasant. There was a strong hint of moustache on her top lip.

Leading the way into an untidy parlour, the woman asked, "Tea or gin, Mr. Williamson?"

"Gin, please. Every time."

"Sensible man," she said. With a change of tone she added, "My fee for a consultation is five pounds."

"That's fine."

"Sit yourself down, Mr. Williamson."

Ben said, being clever, "Look, my name isn't really Williamson."

The woman laughed heartily. She put a hand under each cavorting breast. "I shouldn't worry about that," she said. "Mine isn't really Madam Zena."

Bemused, Ben sat at a table. He had expected to win admiration for being, apparently, so honest. While the woman poured straight gins he told her his name was Arthur Wilton and that he managed an appliance shop in Tooting.

He finished, "I don't know why I gave you a false name."

"People often do. Cheers."

"Cheers."

Madam Zena joined him at the table. After sipping her drink she asked, "So what can I do for you?"

"Mind control," Ben said.

"Mmm?"

"You know, extra-sensory perception."

"Yes? What about it?" She was looking at him closely. He

got the idea that she had been watching him without a break ever since she had opened the door.

He put his elbows on the table. "Look. A friend of mine, he's been doing little experiments in ESP, and I've got the idea there's something sinister about it."

"What nonsense."

"Is it? That's good. You see, I know nothing about this sort of thing. That's why I came. Can you explain ESP to me, please?"

"In a word—no. I can't, and no one else can. There's no empirical evidence. However, I do have an excellent theory. Science prefers to pretend that ESP isn't there."

"What's its history?"

"It's been around for donkey's years. Been in and out of favour. It's also called mental radio, mind-reading, telepathy and thought-transference, as you know."

"That's just it, I don't," Ben said. "I don't know a thing about the supernatural."

The woman gave a scoffing toss of her head, shook it slowly and then took a drink of gin. Putting her glass down with a thud she said,

"Mr. Wilton, do get this notion of the sinister out of your mind. And forget the supernatural. That's for religious people to believe in. There's only the natural."

"Er—meaning?"

"Psychology. It's all psychology. The last frontier left to man. Freud was to the mind what the Wright Brothers were to space travel. All of us, we're dithering around the borders, trying to find the right visa."

Ben asked, "Then what's your theory on ESP?" He was thinking that Madam Zena was not quite as ordinary as she appeared, not quite as mundane as she acted. He felt less comfortable.

"Look here," the woman said. "This is not so hard to accept if you believe in instinct."

"I do, of course."

"Naturally. And this is the same sort of thing. It is known that primitive cultures all had the same themes running through their art and legends. These were peoples who couldn't possibly have been in contact, either because of distance or time. From that we get the theory of collective memory. Are you with me?"

Ben nodded. He thought that there was something belligerent now in the woman's attitude. His discomfort grew.

"I follow that theory with the so-called supernatural. The unconscious of all of us is connected to one memory. In a sense, we share one mind. The gifted, or those who've practiced hard, they can go into that mass and out again to another individual. Identical twins do it with the greatest of ease."

"I see."

"It's a fine thought, that, there being one state of knowing, remembering, understanding. And do you know what I call that state?"

"No."

The woman leaned forward, her face blank of expression. She said, "God."

Ben said, "Oh."

"And God, young man, is love."

Ben nodded uneasily. He drained his glass, looked around the room to avoid the woman's stare, and asked, "Why do you call yourself a clairvoyant if you don't believe in the supernatural?"

"The word means clear-sighted. That's me. I see, and I tell people what they want to know, and sometimes what they don't want to know. If it makes them happy to believe in the occult—fine."

Ben cleared his throat. The woman was still leaning forward, staring, her face blank.

"It's all psychology," she said. "It's that, and nothing else, that tells me certain things about you, young man."

Ben's smile was not a success. He was feeling more uncomfortable by the second. "What things?"

"That you are cold, that you are egocentric to a manic degree, that you are a good liar, and that you are not at all disturbed by the sinister."

Ben let the smile go. It was a moment before he answered with a feeble, "Hardly flattering."

The woman finished her drink and got up. "There will be no charge for the consultation, young man. Good night."

The next evening, wearing jeans and a sweater, Jill got behind the wheel of her Hillman and slammed the door. She asked, "All set?"

Ben nodded. "Away we go."

Jill felt a curious shyness about being the driver, about being in control while Ben sat in the passenger seat. Although sure that he was not one of those males who were critical of women motorists, she found herself driving with unusual care and attention as she steered out of the kerb and moved along Cheever Street.

To divert herself, she asked about the Jaguar. "Is it going to be a big job?"

"Oh no. A few days. As long as it takes to get a new part sent from the factory."

"Expensive, though."

"Still under guarantee," Ben said. "Even so, it's costing me a fortune in taxies."

"I'll bet." Jill glanced at him as she spoke.

Again, as earlier at the door, she was taken by how different Ben looked in a sailing cap and dark glasses. She had thought, with amusement, that he could have played the part of an arms smuggler—leaving her flat carrying the canvas-wrapped rifle and outside glancing in all directions.

"Turn here," Ben said.

She took the corner, after making sure her signalling was correct. "Where're we going anyway?"

"Out beyond Cranwell. I know a quiet place where we can have a bit of shooting."

"We're getting to be quite the sporting types."

"That we are."

"And what *is* that paper, Ben?" Jill asked, nodding toward his feet, where lay what seemed to be a rolled magazine.

"You'll see," he said lightly, giving the same answer as before. "What a beautiful evening."

For half an hour, Ben giving directions, they drove among the exodus traffic. Mostly they chatted about the landmarks that Ben pointed out. He acted almost like a courier. He repeated place-names, and more than once said, "It would be hard to lose your way on this trip."

The last time Ben commented on their surroundings was after they had forked to the right at an isolated telephone booth. They were in real country now, quiet winding lanes with only scattered buildings.

Ben said, "Slow down, Jill. I'll show you my favourite tree. There. There it is." He pointed to the left ahead.

It was an oak, old but stately, spreading thick branches out to canopy the lane. "Gorgeous," Jill said.

"I call it Charles."

"After the king who hid in an oak to escape the Round-heads?"

"Yes. Good for you."

Jill felt cozy and clever. She was forced to add, however, "But don't ask me which Charles it was. I flopped at history."

Ben seemed to find that irrelevant. He said, "I always have a look at Charles when I come by this way."

"He's very handsome."

"Actually, I know the people who live beyond those trees."

"It's charming out here. So peaceful."

Ben looked at his watch. "We'd better get a move on, I think. Won't be too long till it's dusk."

Jill pressed her foot down on the accelerator. Ben began to talk about his Jaguar as he bent to re-tie a shoelace.

After that he was silent. Knowing he was enjoying seeing the scenery as a passenger, Jill kept quiet also. She had relaxed now, felt no need to drive like an efficient robot.

Presently, Jill found herself musing about art galleries. It was ages since she had been to one. With Ben being so much the cerebral type, it might be an idea to suggest they do the Tate or the National together one of these days. Or better still, less professionally and more fun, there was the outdoor show along the park railings on Bayswater Road.

Jill's musing ended as a dog dashed in front of the car. She avoided it neatly, and she and Ben both laughed.

A moment later, Jill's recollection of a dog she had once owned stopped when she switched abruptly to wondering if she should get her hair cut short. It was quite fashionable now, that boyish look. There were even some models with crewcuts. Short hair was definitely going to be the in thing.

Next, Jill began to think about cottages.

There was still an hour of daylight left when they made a final turn beside a railway embankment. Jill steered along a rutted track. The Hillman bounced and squeaked. A line of trees forced the track away from the man-made ridge. Jill was glad. She didn't like being towered over by the high embankment.

"Here," Ben said. "This'll do."

Jill stopped the car. She got out, stretched, strolled around to the passenger side. This was a quiet place, as Ben had said. There were not even birds in the tall trees. Opposite them and the embankment, trash-scattered emptiness stretched away into the distance.

Ben had alighted and taken the canvas off the gun, which he handed to Jill, "Careful. It's loaded."

"Am I having first try?"

"Certainly," he said. He got his mysterious roll from the car and moved toward the embankment. He stopped there by a tree and then went from sight behind its thick trunk.

A moment later he called, "Here's the target."

Into view from behind the tree came a life-size figure of a man. Cut out of heavy, black paper, it was being held up on a stick, to which Ben had fixed the head.

Jill felt a slight queasiness. She called, "What am I supposed to do?"

"Aim at the chest. See how many times out of nine you can hit it. Just aim and keep pulling the trigger."

"It's a weird-looking thing, Ben."

"Yes, I think I did rather well. It wasn't easy."

"Oh, you did very well," Jill said. "Very well indeed. It's a bit too lifelike, that's all."

"It's only paper, Jill. Come on."

Delaying, she asked, "What about distance? How far should I be from the target?"

"You're just right. About twenty paces."

It occurred to Jill how strange this was, talking to someone she couldn't see. The answers might have been coming from the black shape.

"He's the enemy soldier," Ben called. "He's coming to kill you, and you have to get him first. Now. Aim and start shooting."

Jill brought the rifle to her shoulder, aligned the sights the way she had been taught, and squeezed the trigger. Of the nine

shots, four holed various parts of the upper target, which
dithered every time it was hit.

Ben came from around the tree and walked forward. Grinning, he congratulated Jill on her skill, and was so complimentary that she forgot her queasy feeling. But she was still
relieved at being able to hand over the gun and say, "You're
on next."

She went to and behind the tree, picked up the stick and
held out the target. Ben fired his nine shots. He made three
hits.

Until the light began to fail they played the game. Ben
insisted on being generous, made Jill take the most turns at
shooting. He said she was the better shot of the two, anyway.
He cheered as on her last try she placed six holes in the region
of the chest. Jill blushed her pleasure.

Driving away over the track, Jill said, "That was fun."

"Yes. We should come out here again, say Thursday evening. Okay with you?"

"Yes. Fine."

"Also," Ben said, "I was going to ask you about Saturday
night. Will you be free?"

"Yes, Ben. I'll be free."

"Good. I was thinking along the lines of something special.
If I could interest you in that."

"You could indeed."

Satisfaction was implied in the way he adjusted his sunglasses. He said, "I'm not even sure I'll be here over the weekend. I'll let you know. Be fun to go out somewhere Saturday
night and live it up."

"Yes," Ben said into the receiver, "Saturday night."

"What a nice idea, old man. The Minstrel Boy, did you
say?"

"Yes, Peter, that old pub near Cranwell. They put on a very good feed."

"So I've heard."

Ben swung around in his chair so that he was looking out of his office window. "The thing is, I'd rather take people out than entertain at home. You know what baching's like."

"That I do," the man said. "Hold on. I'll have a natter with the little woman."

That phrase made Ben cringe. Come to that, he thought, Peter and Ann Cape were both cringe-makers, what with their baby talk and naïveté, and their conviction that the kennels they operated were of great interest to everybody. But the Capes were steady, real pillars, respectable to the last neat fold. They would do nicely.

Peter Cape came back on the line. "Yes, old man, we've nothing on. Saturday it is."

Ben smiled and hung up.

That was Wednesday afternoon. During the rest of the business hours he was too busy to make other personal calls—he had already made five in his search for the solid and available. At four-thirty he left the bank and went to the underground garage.

Driving out, it occurred to Ben, as it had that morning, that there was always a longshot possibility of being seen in his Jaguar by someone who knew someone who happened to know Jill Parr. It was a small world.

So? he thought. So nothing. Should the longshot come off, he would say the Jaguar agency had loaned him a car almost identical to his own. Smooth.

At home Ben started making telephone calls. The second was successful: The Dixons were free Saturday night and would be delighted to be his guests at the Minstrel Boy. They, like the Capes, were the epitome of middle-class respectability.

Ben poured himself a weak gin and tonic. He went out onto

his balcony, sprawled in a chair and surveyed the panorama, the urban spread made golden by a sinking sun.

While sipping his drink, with his free hand he touched his chin, neck, shoulder, ribs, thighs. He had rarely felt so at one with himself, so contented.

Later, dressed in his tuxedo, he drove to Mayfair and dined at the most expensive restaurant he knew of.

Next morning at work, Ben several times found the opportunity to pass near the closed door of Harry Farnsworth's office. When he at last heard voices from in there, instead of the previous silence, he tapped on the door and eased it open.

"Hello, Harry. Spare one minute?"

"One, yes," Farnsworth said. "I'm a slave this morning." He was semi-sitting on the edge of his desk. He held a cigarette whose ash was an inch long. It formed the point of fascinated attention of a middle-aged woman who sat nearby with pad and pencil.

"Saturday night," Ben said. "I'm trying to get a little bash together. Will you and Val be free?"

Harry Farnsworth frowned, flicked a glance at his secretary, asked, "What was that again?"

Ben ignored the implication: You should know better than to come in here now with social doings. Blandly he repeated his question.

"Free, yes," Harry huffed. "But we like to slop around on weekends, except for having people in for drinks Sunday noon. You know that."

Ben pretended to notice the secretary, who was still staring at the downcurved cigarette ash. He said, "Oh look, I'll get back to you about this later. Sorry to interrupt." He retreated and closed the door.

Ben gave a short, sprightly hum on returning to his own office. The visit had polished two facets of his scheme. One, he had established that the Farnsworths would, as expected, be at home on Saturday night; two, the secretary could bear witness to the fact that he had wanted Harry and Val as his guests.

The rest of the morning passed swiftly. At noon Ben joined two of his colleagues in a pub for lunch—beer and a one-plate special. He talked about the boredom of banking work.

The afternoon was unusually busy, which suited Ben. It passed time and kept him from stimulating thought. He was one of the last to leave the building. On the way home he stopped for coffee and sandwiches.

Later he changed into casual clothes, in the pockets of which were the sailing cap and sunglasses. Again leaving the Jaguar behind, he took a cab to Cheever Street. During the ride he put on glasses and cap.

Jill was ready. They came down straight away to the Hillman, Ben carrying the canvas-wrapped gun. The target, that was already there, had been left under the seat.

The outing was a repeat of Tuesday. By mentioning landmarks Ben made sure that Jill would remember this particular route; he had her slow by the oak tree which he had christened Charles for her benefit—and this time he pointed out a gap in the hedge. He bent in pretence of fiddling with his lace while they were passing the cottage gate—you never knew, Val or Harry could be strolling there. By the railway embankment he let Jill have the most turns at shooting at the man-size target.

Ben was satisfied. Neither himself nor his car had been seen recently in the vicinity of the Farnsworth place. Jill knew her way there. She had become a reasonably proficient shot.

On the drive back, Ben concentrated on making Jill feel more at home with the rifle. Repeatedly he put into her mind that it was a fine and attractive piece of craftsmanship, not really dangerous at all.

At the Cheever Street flat, while they were having a nightcap, Jill said, "It's time I gave Dad's gun a polish."

Ben watched happily while Jill, with oil and furniture

cream, worked over the rifle and commented on the beauty of its yellow wood and matt black metal. She went on for so long that he began to get bored.

"That's enough," he said finally.

Jill looked up with a blink. Ben realised that he had sounded too commanding. He smiled, "You'll wear the damn thing out. Here, let me put it away for you."

"Thanks, Ben."

He took gun and canvas into her bedroom. Quickly, silently, he loaded the magazine from his dwindling stock of shells. He slid the canvas roll into place and put the gun in its wardrobe corner.

Jill insisted on driving him home. On the way, enjoying his cunning at diverting Jill's attention, Ben dropped the remaining dozen-odd bullets out of the window.

They stopped by the entrance to the tall modern block. Jill said, "Wow, what a slum."

Given any encouragement, Ben thought, she would be inviting herself in. He got out with the rolled target and said, "About Saturday. I'll be in touch."

"Right, Ben."

"It might not be until the last minute, so be sure of being alone and ready, eh?"

"I will."

He leaned inside and kissed her. "Good night."

"Night, Ben. Thanks for a fun evening."

Inside the building, going up, Ben wiped the lipstick from his mouth. His final act of the night was to tear into small pieces the target, now ragged, and flush them a handful at a time down the toilet.

Friday was another busy day, and again Ben was glad. He gave himself fully to the paperwork and the two interviews with loan seekers, and even stayed at his desk during lunchtime, having rolls and coffee sent in.

Standing by his door at four-thirty, Ben heard Harry Farnsworth leave. He himself left five minutes later. In the street Ben kept going when he came to the mouth of the underground garage. He felt in need of a walk and a think. Everything was set for the following night, but he wanted to go over the scheme in detail, poke for flaws.

Hands afted, chin lowered, oblivious to the bustle around him, Ben mused:

It's eight o'clock on Saturday. I park the car within sight of Jill's house. I give her the urge to get the gun and go out. This I could do from a distance, which would be safer, but I want to see her leave, to make sure she's on her way—some accident or other occurrence could keep her in the house.

Jill in her car, I take off fast. I use the shortest way to the Cranwell area while she is on a longer one. I stop at least twice to concentrate and keep her urge alive. I go to the Minstrel Boy. The others will be there already because they were given an earlier time, That to rule out social lateness. Before going in, I order Jill to stop at the spot she knows so well by now. Inside the pub, I greet the guests, chat, excuse myself and go to wash my hands. In the lavatory I go in a stall for sure privacy so that I can concentrate hard for the few minutes needed to finish it off.

Good, Ben thought. No flaws so far. Jill and himself and the alibi guests, they were fine. But what about the passive protagonist, Harry Farnsworth? And Val. Didn't their end of it need a little investigating? Timing being of the essence, how did his fit in with theirs?

Ben knew that the Farnsworth weekend began Friday. Tonight would therefore be the same as Saturday. So, he mused, a dress rehearsal for them ought to be arranged. Also, that would get him dead accurate as to darkness, let him know if he should shave or add five minutes. For one thing, it wouldn't do for the cottage's outside light to be switched on.

Ben turned and headed back. The bank still being open, he would go to his office and shove some papers in a briefcase. After that, a meal and a telephone call to Harry and then a run out to visit him, playing the worried underling.

It was a quarter to eight when Ben steered his Jaguar through the white gateway. He went to the gravel turnabout and parked beside the Rover. Carrying his briefcase he got out.

The presence here of the Rover, ungaraged, made Ben glad he had decided on this dry run. The same with the fact of the gate being wide open. What if someone drove in at the wrong moment, or if Harry came out to garage his car?

Ben went to the cottage door. His knock was answered by Harry's call of, "Come in." Ben let himself into the hall.

Farnsworth, a scruffy bohemian, came through the open kitchen doorway. His smile was polite, not welcoming. That was the way he had sounded on the telephone.

Ben said, "Hi. Did you know you'd left your gate open?"

"Always do. It doesn't mattter. People know better than to bother us."

Fine, Ben thought. "Except me," he said. "Sorry about this."

Harry waved Ben ahead of him into the living room. He asked, "You know what happens to people who take their work home with them?"

"No."

"They get twin ulcers."

"Harry, as I told you on the phone, this is a bit tricky. I'm not the type for worrying out of school, you know that."

"Well, yes."

"Nor would I have bothered you here. You have enough of this nonsense all through the week."

Harry grunted. He indicated a chair. "Sit down. Drink?"

"Well, maybe a small Scotch." Ben sat and put the case on his knees. Surreptitiously he glanced at his watch before starting to unfasten straps.

He said, "By the way, the Rover's still outside. I suppose you put it away when it begins to get dark."

Harry uncorked a bottle. "I leave it. Weekends I pretend the car doesn't exist."

Fine again, Ben thought. He rustled in the briefcase.

Val Farnsworth came in while her husband was still at the drinks cabinet. "Hi, Ben," she said. "I thought I heard the Jag. Don't get up."

"Hello, Val. Thanks."

There was a meeting of eyes. Though short, it had intensity. To Ben it spoke a saga. He felt that familiar hollowness inside. Val looked so desirable in paint-splashed shirt and jeans that he felt his body jerk spontaneously as it reacted, made as if to move over there, claim, hold.

"What?" Ben asked. He looked up to see Harry beside him with a drink. "Oh, thanks."

"Cheers. Something for you, Val?"

"No, dear, thanks. Not when I'm working."

"I'm not having anything either."

"Ben, are you staying for supper?"

"God, no," he said. "It's bad enough that I've come to bother you with all this."

Harry Farnsworth put his hands on his hips. "Right. Tell uncle the big problem."

Ben brought out a sheaf of papers, a mangle of bent corners and paper-clipped attachments. "The Potterson loan."

"Yes, but what exactly? You were pretty vague about it on the telephone."

"I'm pretty vague now, if it comes to that," Ben said. "There's something here that I can't put my finger on." He looked up from the papers, turning from one to the other of his hosts.

"Oh, but look. I'm keeping you from things."

Val shrugged. Her husband said an unenthusiastic, "That's all right."

"No. Listen. I'll tell you what. You two go on with what you were doing. Meanwhile, I'll go through this junk and see if I can get my ideas sorted out."

Harry brightened. "Fair enough."

"In fact, it'll probably take half an hour or more, so just leave me to it, eh?"

Val said, "If it's going to take that long, you might as well stay to eat something with us."

Ben looked down so that his feelings wouldn't show: gratitude, and understanding of her desire to keep him here as long as possible.

Harry Farnsworth, all host now, said, "Help yourself to booze, old son."

"Thanks. Don't worry about me. I'll give you a shout when I'm ready."

Val left the room first. She always did that when the three of them were together. Ben knew that it was because she was afraid, if alone with him, of being unable to hold back any longer from expressing her love.

After bringing forward a coffee table for the papers, Harry also left. He closed the door.

Ben sagged back in the armchair and smiled lazily. The privacy was an unexpected bonus. He hadn't imagined that he would be left alone. Now he could work on it properly, time every thought. There would be no doubts about the outcome.

He checked his watch, got up and took the glass of whisky over to a potted plant beside the rear French windows. Into the pot he emptied his glass. He wanted his head to be perfectly clear. The same tomorrow night.

Seeing the papers on the coffee table as he turned, Ben reminded himself that there would be no problems, no suspicion. The Potterson loan was blue-ribbon. Later, he would say he had got the wording wrong. He'd had a lot of worry for nothing. They'd have a good laugh about it.

With frequent glances at his watch, Ben strolled around the room. He thought of himself getting dressed in his latest suit for the evening at the Minstrel Boy; himself driving the Jaguar; himself turning into Cheever Street and stopping well back from the house; himself checking his wristwatch.

He did that now in reality. The second hand was coming up to eight o'clock. Ben returned to his chair, sat down and put his fingertips to his temples.

Jill was ironing a dress. She worked back and forth over the material with strokes that comforted in their rhythm and repetition. An added charm was the knowledge that this chore was for weekend play, not Monday work; that, in point, she was not, as so often before, wishing the time-free hiatus behind her.

Roll on tomorrow night, Jill thought. She pressed with happy caution along the edge of a seam.

Having no idea what Ben had in mind for Saturday—slick or casual, town or country—Jill had decided to be wholly prepared. On five minutes' notice she would be able to put on this dress or a shortie evening gown, a trouser suit or jeans, or stay as she was now, in skirt and blouse.

Jill paused in her work. She lifted the iron. Slowly she looked around the kitchen.

A notion had just come to her.

Raising her chin Jill thought: Dumb. Stupid. For one thing, I don't feel like going out. For another, Ben might call about tomorrow night. For a third, to set off on a shooting trip at this time of the evening, even if accompanied, would be foolish, as there wasn't more than half an hour of good light left.

Jill said aloud, "I don't care that much for shooting the rifle anyway. Honest."

It seemed, oddly, as though she were having to convince herself. Giving a short laugh, she went back to ironing.

Her movements were awkward. It looked as if she was aware of being watched or was trying to be natural for a home movie. She was not conscious of glancing again around the room.

The notion was persisting. It had a persuasive quality. Jill found herself less in opposition. Not, she told herself, that she was going to follow the curious inclination, but she wouldn't dismiss it out of hand.

The notion ebbed, flowed, ebbed.

Jill set down the iron on its rack. Moving to the gas stove she put a light under the kettle. "A good cup of tea," she said. "Tea works wonders." She smiled. Her eyes were not part of the smile.

The notion thrived.

Jill, fighting, made herself busy switching off and unplugging the iron, putting her dress on a hanger, folding up the damp cloth, taking . . .

Jill stopped moving, stopped fighting. The smile-shape went from her mouth. Disquieted, she let the notion come through without hindrance.

It was not, she told herself, really that foolish. Why should she sit here all evening on the off-chance of getting a call from Ben. He wouldn't be hurt to find her out. He would call again later or tomorrow. He had, after all, said that it would probably be one of those last minute things.

Jill stood there perplexed, the ironing board semi-folded. Her emotions were in a slow, turgid whirl. She didn't know if she was content or alarmed. She did know she was anxious: Was it better to give in to her own wishes, or to resist them for some strange reason?

In the cottage, Ben sat up straight. He had not, he realised, been concentrating the way he would on the actual occasion. There were faint noises from the kitchen and he was conscious of the nearness of Val, in her studio.

Ben rose. He went to the French windows and looked up at the extension to the house. There was no window on this side. There was nothing to see. He was wasting his time.

Striding back to the armchair, Ben reminded himself that tomorrow night there would be far more and far stronger diversions: traffic, people, lights and noise. He had to forget Harry, forget Val.

He sat and pressed the flat of his palms to his head. He settled to profound concentration.

Jill had put the ironing things away. The kettle was eking out the first whispers of steam.

"I don't think I'll bother with tea," she said. She went over to the stove and switched off the gas flame. "Out you go. And I'm going to keep on talking aloud. Everyone does it."

The notion seemed to have faded.

Her hands held at her waist in the pose of prayer, Jill walked into the main room. She thought how good it was that she had been talking to herself aloud; and then she raised her eyebrows as she began to do exactly the reverse.

Go out. Take the gun. Get in the car and start driving.

Jill came to a stop. Her hands she changed to an interlocking of fingers.

Take the rifle out to the car. You know which way to go. It'll be fun. The gun's loaded. You can have nine fast shots.

It was a beautiful evening, Jill told herself. A shame really to spend it indoors. There might be a sunset later. If the light's gone so that it's too late for shooting, that won't matter.

"It'll be fun," she said aloud.

Her anxiety seemed to lessen as she went along to her bedroom. She looked in the wardrobe. The notion faded, then returned. She took hold of the canvas bundle and lifted it out.

Get the rifle.

"I have it," Jill said, almost snapping the words. Her voice was high.

Get the rifle.

Jill gripped the bundle with both hands as well as pressing it to her stomach. "I've got it. It's here. What's wrong with me?"

Take the gun. Get in the car. Start driving.

Jill lifted the rifle into her arms and went along to the door of the flat. Letting herself out, she started down. With every step she took she felt less troubled. She opened the front door. She burst out of the house and immediately had a sense of release.

Go out and get in the car. Take the gun and go out.

"I am, I am," Jill said plaintively.

She hurried through the gate and along to her Hillman. She opened the door and tossed the rifle onto the back seat, got in behind the wheel and took the keys from their hiding place—a magnet under the sun visor.

Get in the car.

Jill sat motionless, staring ahead.

Get in the car and drive. It will be fun.

She said, "I know the way."

Starting the motor, Jill wondered why she'd had that foolish notion to stay home.

Ben lowered his hands and looked at his watch. It showed seven minutes past eight. He mused that seven minutes should be ample, that by this time Saturday he would be seeing Jill Parr coming out of the house with the gun.

Normally it would take less time, Ben knew. But Jill would put up fair resistance to leaving, naturally, because she would be expecting him to call about the date he had mentioned. On the other hand, she would be all ready to go out, would have no need of preparation. Seven minutes was about right.

Next, Ben thought, as soon as Jill had moved off in the Hillman, he would drive away himself.

Still with his eyes on the watch, Ben settled down to the job of picturing the road he would take tomorrow night. He saw the Jaguar as it met each set of traffic lights, each well-known stretch of road, each landmark, taking these in sequence at a steady pace.

Ben was conscientious. He didn't try to skip from one part to another. There was too much at stake. The future happiness of himself and Val.

When the time was coming close to a quarter past eight, Ben searched ahead on the short-cut way he was recalling. He pictured a lay-by in front of a row of suburban shops. It would be ideal for his purpose.

In imagination, Ben steered his Jaguar into the lay-by, halted and began to concentrate. In reality, he put his hands back to his temples and thought, slowly:

That's it. Keep driving. How good it is to be out. The roads are nice and quiet even if it is Saturday night. This is fun.

After a repeat of that he looked at the time. The bout of encouragement had taken thirty seconds. He thought it would be better to make it one minute on the actual occasion. There was no point in rushing things.

On the other hand, Ben mused, there would be no sense in having created for Jill the long way round if he himself was going to dawdle on his own route. But still. One minute.

Ben went back to imagining the trip. He pictured the Jaguar pulling out of the lay-by (even allowing a pause for a bus to pass) and then began to visualise the road.

This he stopped, however, on realising that he could pick the route up again by, say, the Esso service station, at twenty-two minutes past eight. That should be about right.

Ben began to think of somewhere this side of the filling station where he could safely make a halt, for concentration. There were several places that—

"That's it," a voice said.

Ben started. He jerked upright from his crouch in the armchair, his heart thudding.

The door of the room was open and Harry Farnsworth stood on the threshold, looking at him. "Sorry," Harry said. "Did I make you jump?"

"It's okay. I didn't hear you."

"Not surprised, old son. I haven't seen anyone so lost in thought for years."

"Yes," Ben said, recovered, nerves and heartbeat back to normal. He smiled. "Really lost."

"No," Jill said out loud. "No, I'm not. I know the way."

But the idea didn't persist. It had, in any case, been as feeble as it was groundless. All the landmarks were there, and now she was passing the mattress factory, which no one could possibly mistake.

Even so, it was peculiar that she kept dwelling on other landmarks, other stretches of highway. Only a minute ago, while on a quiet street of houses, she had started to think about that big Esso station further west.

"Petrol," Jill said. "I'm worried about running out." She glanced at the fuel gauge and tapped it with her knuckles. It showed three-quarters full.

"So that's all right. It's just silly worrisome me. And what's more, today is Friday, not Saturday."

"Deep in it, eh?" Farnsworth asked.

"And getting somewhere," Ben said.

"Great."

"Yes, Harry, I'm really nailing it down."

"Good man. Don't let me interrupt. I just came in to draw the curtains. Be dusk soon."

"Yes?"

Harry Farnsworth went over to the front window. "In fact, it's dusk now."

"Good," Ben said, and quickly hid that by asking, "Keeping yourself busy in the kitchen?"

"Like anything. You should take up this cooking game. It's a real lark."

"Poached eggs on toast. That's my speed."

Farnsworth settled the drapes and moved away. He went toward the rear of the room, passing behind Ben, who, enjoying himself, asked,

"What are you going to be cooking tomorrow night?"

"Chinese deal. All bits and bobs. Great fun."

"Fun to eat, yes."

Harry drew the curtains across the French windows and turned. "Which reminds me. Weren't you planning something for Saturday?"

"I'm going to make it the middle of the week," Ben said. He added, in case Harry mentioned it to Val, "I think."

"Mid-week's more our style, old son." He switched on a lamp, bringing a warm glow to the room.

Without thinking of the action, Ben looked at his watch. Farnsworth said a grinned, "Don't worry, I'm off. I wouldn't dream of spoiling your pleasure."

"You're all heart, Harry."

"That I am." On his way back across the room he brought another lamp to life.

Ben said, casually, "Don't forget the outside light over the front door. "

Farnsworth shook his head. "No electricity gets wasted around here. We only put that one on when we're expecting people."

Lovely, Ben thought.

"See you," the host said. He went out and closed the door behind him.

The time, Ben saw, was twenty-one minutes past eight. He set to work. He imagined himself at the wheel of the Jaguar as it was moving past an Esso station, then circling a traffic island, then turning off onto a residential street and slowing to a stop.

The houses, he mused, would have their windows curtained, like here. No one would see the driver with his head in his hands. And if anyone did, so what? Nothing strange about that. The driver could have a headache, he could be looking at a map, he could have grit in his eyes. Perfectly normal.

Ben, acting the part of his Saturday evening self in the Jaguar, lowered head to hands and thought: Keep going. That's the way. You couldn't make a mistake on this road, you know it so well. Keep going.

Dusk was playing hazy games with visibility. The buildings appeared to have a predatory lean outward. Neon signs had ghost edges. Stores were bright and some of the passing cars had their lights on.

Jill wondered about the lights of the Hillman. In fact, for some time now she had been thinking about lighting and curtains. Mixed up in that had been ideas of food.

"Am I hungry?" Jill mused aloud. She changed gear to pass a slow-moving car. "Should I stop somewhere and get something to eat? No. But what about that other thing?"

Jill found that she didn't know whether she should switch on the headlights or not. She did tend fractionally toward the latter. There had been a feeling of satisfaction along with the knowledge that something was unlit. What, she didn't know. Perhaps she had been recalling that she had turned the flame off under the kettle.

Her only urge at the moment was to keep driving. She had

been doing that anyway, and still was. But abruptly now came the idea that she should be driving with more . . . more something. Yes, but what? Intensity? Interest?

Perhaps speed, she thought. She had been going fairly slow, it was true. And yes, of course, the dusk. It had reminded her that she had to hurry. And that didn't make sense.

The last thought Jill ignored. She wasn't going to get involved. She pressed her foot down on the power. The Hillman shuddered its usual complaint at having to work, yet responded.

It careened on. Directly ahead, a lumbering truck grew quickly large in Jill's vision. The advertising slogan swelled bigger and bigger. Exhaust fumes surged in at the open window.

At the last moment, Jill twisted the steering wheel. She swerved out and went alongside the truck and felt a slight skid as she over-corrected. Cutting in again, she heard the angry blast of a horn.

Jill was unmoved. She felt devoid of emotion. Her anxiety, that had gone long ago. She was calm. Matchingly, her face was blank. She might have been passively watching a play in which she had lost interest.

Her thoughts were mainly weak and fleeting. Even those few that came strongly were often nonsensical. In addition to food, lighting and curtains, she had thought of maps, a headache, Ben's Jaguar, the danger of getting dust in her eyes.

And now there was this urge to keep going.

"I am," Jill said. "Damn it, I am. What else can I do?"

She saw a set of traffic lights ahead. They were on red. She went toward them with no reduction in speed. As she reached the junction, the yellow came on. She was unconcerned.

When, a moment later, Jill allowed her foot to ease up on the accelerator, it was not because of any sensation of danger in respect of the cars she was swerving around, both on the inside and the outside. It was because her urge to keep pressing forward had faded.

Now she had that quiet, continuing desire to obey her wishes, fanciful or not; to go out to the railway embankment and practice shooting. She felt sure that the dusk didn't matter. The area out there was probably as bright as day. She must have noticed lamps without registering the fact consciously.

Jill turned a corner and came onto a quieter stretch of road. There were few cars. One, approaching, flashed its lights at her so strongly that she had to put a hand in front of her face to kill the glare.

She drove on without doing what she normally would have done: make a comment, in thought or word or shout, as to the other driver's bad manners. By the time her hand was back on the wheel, she had forgotten the incident.

Into Jill's mind filtered the concept that all this was being imagined. She was actually sitting at home, on the couch with her legs curled under. She was day-dreaming about being here in the car. Soon she would snap out of it, get up and go to make herself a cup of tea.

The concept left as easily as it had arrived.

Dimly Jill saw on the sidewalk a man being tugged along by a large dog, and dimly was aware of the man shouting something at her as she went by.

She came to a shopping district. The stores, though closed, were all brightly lit. For some reason she found herself thinking of a wristwatch. The shops were left behind.

Next, every nerve in Jill's body jumped. With a roar, a figure had erupted into view on the road beside her. She instinctively leaned away. The car swerved. She corrected.

By now she had recognized the figure as a man on a motorcycle. He was still there, keeping pace. He was in uniform and helmeted. It was a policeman.

Above the roar of his machine he shouted, "Lights!"

Jill gasped, "What?"

"Put your lights on, lady!"

"Oh, yes," she muttered. "Sorry." She sent a nervous hand to the dashboard, found the switch by touch, turned it down. The road in front of her sprang to brightness.

The motor-cycle policeman waved and went roaring on.

Jill eased down again to calm and dullness. She drove at a steady speed. Traffic was reduced to the occasional car; the air breezing in at the open window was sweeter.

Jill left the heavily built-up area behind. The road narrowed. Houses were thinning out, and soon they were seen only as sparse spots of light in the surrounding darkness. Road lamps had ended.

Jill drove along a winding lane with hedges on either side. It was not familiar. But she reminded herself that she had not been on this route after dark, at least not in this direction. Even so, she began to feel she had come the wrong way.

Then she saw a landmark up ahead. It was a telephone booth on a fork in the lane.

Stop by the tree, Ben thought, his fingertips kneading his temples. Stop by the tree called Charles. You must stop there and draw close into the side.

In reality, Ben was sitting on the seat-edge of an armchair in the Farnsworth living room. In imagination, he was standing by his Jaguar, which he had parked with other vehicles behind the Minstrel Boy. The country pub's parking lot was dim and deserted. Nearby were the two cars belonging to the friends who were his guests tonight. They were safely inside.

Stop by Charles. You must stop there.

The parking lot and the pub dissolved as Ben lowered his hands. He checked the time. It was right on, he thought. Perhaps a little ahead as far as Jill was concerned. Better to give her another couple of minutes.

Ben got up from the chair. Hands comfortably clasped behind, he began to stroll around the room. He felt tall and fine, strong and wise. He felt, in a way, noble.

Ben went back to considering the actions of his pawn, Jill Parr, now in respect of aftermath.

All that was up to her, he thought. From the conclusion of the killing onward, she would be a free agent, for it was unlikely that he would have the time or opportunity to indulge in mind-control. But it wasn't needed. So what would she do?

Jill would drive home. She would take the gun into the flat and put it away. She would go to bed. The evening would be over. She may never connect herself with the death of a person she had never heard of in a house she didn't know, nor was anyone else likely to make such a connexion. If she did suspect, even a hint's worth, all the better. Petrified, she would keep her mouth tightly clamped.

And, Ben mused, what about being suspected from the other side? Well, hopefully the only clue would be the car, should someone going by—an unlikely event—see the Hillman parked there. That someone would not of course take the number, and might not even be able to recall the make, let alone the fact of it being old, green and a convertible. After all, it was only later that the car would become significant.

But say the worst happened. Say the police traced the Hillman to Jill. That she had been dating a colleague of the murdered man would vastly intrigue the police. But that colleague would be clean, and astounded. Guns? Practicing shooting? No, he knew nothing about it. Jill would be on her own.

Ben smiled. As far as his relationship with Jill was concerned, that was over. They'd had their last date. If all went well, he would never see her again. There would be another woman in his life. A real one.

Ben quickly stopped himself from thinking about Val. He glanced at the cocktail cabinet, decided not to chance a drink

—he needed that clear head—and returned to the matter of the police investigation.

As Jill would most certainly never come under suspicion, her car unseen, the detectives would be hung up on the question of motive. It was too bad they wouldn't be getting a ready-made one, as on the first scheme. But you couldn't have everything.

Ben thought that the police would have to take whatever they could find: business enemy, some desperate bankrupt who had been refused a loan, husband of one of his floozies, a homicidal maniac.

Still circling the room, Ben nodded. He liked the girl idea best. And it didn't have to be only jealousy. It could be an angry father of some girl that Harry had got pregnant—the police, of course, they wouldn't know of Harry's impotence. It could be a girl's boy friend whose intention had been merely to frighten, not kill. It could even be one of the girls herself, a cast-off mistress, the hell-hath-no-fury syndrome.

Ben jiggled his clasped hands with pleasure. He had realised that, on the outside chance of Jill Parr becoming involved, a possible motive would be that she had been Harry's girl friend. That would stop the police from searching elsewhere.

Either way, Ben decided, during the investigation he would make a point of letting slip to the detectives about the dead man's long history of extra-marital relations.

Next, Ben came to a halt in his circling as it occurred to him, painfully, that Val might be suspected. She would be on the scene, to start with. The theory could be that she had found out about all her husband's women, and had killed him through rage, or through a fear of him wanting a divorce. So was it wise to mention the girl friends?

Also, Ben mused, there was another danger for Val. She might at some time in the past have been distraught enough to tell a close friend about the passion she had for her husband's younger colleague, and that friend might repeat it to the police. Theory: Val had killed Harry in order to be free.

Ben shook his head fretfully. But a moment later he smiled and walked on again. He had got the answer to the problem of Val's safety. He would arrange to have her out of the way.

Tomorrow night, Ben thought, a telephone call could be made at seven or seven-thirty. He would disguise his voice. Some emergency had come up. Or perhaps something genuine. It wouldn't really matter, just so long as it got her away from the house.

Ben knew that an idea for the ruse would come to him. There was ample time to chew on that minor problem. Now he had to get back to the main task.

Returning to his chair, Ben sat and looked at his watch. First the outdoors again, he thought, then inside to meet the guests briefly before going to the washroom for the final push.

He re-created the scene on the Minstrel Boy parking lot, saw himself standing there with hands to his temples. He did that in reality.

Stop by the Charles tree, he thought. You must pull into the side there and stop.

Jill was bemused.

For the past five minutes or more she had been sitting here in the car. She had followed her wishes and parked here in the side of the lane by the big oak. But then she had gone on telling herself to do exactly that. Switching off the motor had made no difference, nor had pulling on the hand-brake.

After that, however, the urge to stop had faded. In its place had come thoughts of a drink, of the police, of girl friends, and of herself. It had been a meaningless jumble.

Stop by the Charles tree. You must pull into the side there and stop.

Jill tensed. She drew her bottom lip between her teeth. She let it out again to say, "Maybe this is the wrong place. The wrong tree. Maybe I should drive on. I've got confused in the dark. I could drive on and look for another tree somewhere else."

Her inner voice was still telling her to stop. She reached for the ignition key, switched on, but paused on fingering the starter button: the urge to stop had again faded.

Switching off, Jill sat on. She was no less bemused. Her calves began to ache with the tension of her legs. She looked at the lane lit by her headlights, at the hedges, at the branches looming overhead.

She questioned what she was doing here. The urge had gone, yes, but she had no desire to move, as before, to keep heading for the railway embankment. So being here must be right. For what purpose?

"I just don't get this at all," Jill said.

She wished she had a cigarette. She wished she felt differently, meaning her normal self—though at this moment she didn't feel too far from that. She wished she knew if this were really happening or if it belonged to imagination.

Into her mind came the picture of a pub's interior. It was like earlier on this outing, when she had seen landmarks that belonged to another route. This pub, it was bright and cheery. People were sitting around a table laughing. There were full glasses.

"Yes," Jill said, "a drink would be nice."

Put your gloves on.

Jill perked. She thought that anything was better than sitting here like a dummy, even if it did mean that she was talking to herself inside again. She said,

"I'll put my gloves on. If the poor old things haven't fallen apart."

Put the gloves on.

Jill took the black kid driving gloves from their ring on the dashboard. Snuggling into them she mused that her hands were going to be uncomfortably warm.

Turn the motor off. Also the headlights.

"The motor is off," Jill said.

She gave a final tug to her gloves and flicked off the lights switch. The immediate blackness was total, so much so that it made her flinch. But within seconds comparative lightness came from the sky. Jill could still see the branches above.

She wondered if . . . but she interrupted herself with, *Get the gun. This is where the target is. You know the way. You'll remember it presently. Get the gun.*

Jill reached behind and picked up the canvas bundle. She brought it to her lap and unrolled it, uncovering the rifle. The canvas she crumpled and let fall to the floor on the passenger side.

Take the gun with you. Get out of the car. Be careful nobody sees you. Those things are illegal. That's nothing to worry over, if you're careful.

Jill got out onto the road. Holding the rifle with both hands, she used her hip to close the door. It swung to with a crash that caused a fluttering of wings somewhere above.

Jill was still giving herself instructions internally. She crossed the lane to the opposite hedge and began looking for the gap she told herself to find. She knew she had been here before and would presently remember details.

Aloud she said, "This is where the target is."

She came to the break in the hedge. There was ample space for her to get through without danger of snagging her clothes on the brambles. One high-reaching step took her to the other side.

Here she was among trees and in a deeper darkness. She knew it would be foolish to venture far from the road. However, the strong inner voice of her reason knew better. It told her to go in and to the right. She did so.

There was just light enough for her to see without shuffling or fumbling her way from trunk to trunk. She shared her gaze between the path ahead and the ground underfoot.

"I know the way," she said.

Now bear slightly left. Keep bearing left. This will all come back to you in a second. This is fun.

"I'm quite all right," Jill said, her voice faint.

There. Now you can see a light ahead of you through the trees.

Jill could see no light. She looked all around. There was only the darkness. She felt the beginnings of panic. Gasping, she blundered forward.

The tree trunk appeared so quickly that she was unable to stop or dodge. Her shoulder hit wood. The collision sent her staggering. She dropped the gun. Herself she kept from falling with a grab at another tree.

Lips trembling, she went swiftly back in a stoop, saw the gun and snatched it up, went on in what she hoped was the same direction as before.

She saw light. It was a pink glimmer and it lay straight ahead. She made for it, going faster, worried, when the thought came, *Here you are. This is it.*

As the trees thinned, the glimmer separated. It was actually two different squares of light, Jill saw, of the same size and on the same level but of different hues and intensities.

The trees ended. Jill stopped short. Her worry went, for she felt that she had arrived, that this was it.

She noted that she was on the edge of a gravel turnabout. Opposite was a house, light showing from behind two curtained windows on the ground floor. Near one end of the house were parked two cars.

*The target will appear when the door opens. You under-
stand now. You knew all along what it would be.*

Jill could make out the shape of the house door, in dimness
between the glowing windows.

*To make the man-size target appear, you have to knock on
the door sharply. You knock, turn, take ten long, fast paces
and then turn again. You bring your gun up into the ready position.*

"I understand now," Jill said.

*Fire as soon as the door opens and the target appears.
That's simple. You know how. Fire and keep on firing.*

Jill started to walk across the gravel. The sound it made underfoot was minimal. She said a toneless, "This is fun."

She came to a halt in front of the door. Lifting her right
hand, clenched, she rapped her knuckles hard on the wood
three times. She turned and began to pace out the way back.

Her inner voice was telling her all over again what she
should do, just as if she had not started. This interfered with
her counting. She had to make a guess about the ten paces. It
was at the centre point on the gravel that she stopped.

She swung around. At the same time she brought the rifle
up to her shoulder. Left eye closed, she sighted on the door's
upper half.

She heard a click from there. The door opened, receded.
Revealed was a dim hallway, light coming into it from the left.
In the frame was a figure.

The door had not stopped moving before Jill squeezed the
trigger. A shot rang out, and then another as she went on
squeezing. The shots came fast, on top of one another. The
last was gone while she was still hearing an echo of the first.

She let the rifle sag. Both eyes open, her vision free of the
sights, she saw the figure swaying back as if in slow motion. It
looked real. Jill had a strange sensation in her stomach.

The figure swayed and drooped, and began to turn as it

made a languid, falling retreat. From there came a scream. It was a male voice that Jill knew. It belonged to Ben.

Jill dropped the rifle and ran.

The drive home was like a sensible nightmare. There was nothing of the fantastic or ludicrous. Because of that it was all the more terrifying.

Jill had no awareness of her hands and feet on the controls. Her attention was given to the world outside the body of her car: the shouted curses and brake-wails, the flashes of headlights, the racing lamps and signs, the vehicles that came hurtling at her with evil intent; and, three times, the bump as kerbs passed under her wheels.

Jill was petrified. And glad to be. She encouraged the terror. She held to it grimly.

The sights and sounds of fear created a heat to counter the cold inside. They kept her from seeing again that drooping body and from hearing the scream. They stopped her recalling that one of the two cars on the turnabout, seen closely as she ran by, was a new Jaguar. They held her back from a full stare at the fact that Ben was shot and that she had done the shooting.

In her fear, Jill was almost gay.

On turning the last corner into Cheever Street, she took it too close. A lamp-post slapped the side of the Hillman, pushed it off and chased it with a sprinkle of glass. Jill went on, saw a parking space, steered in and smacked to a rocking halt.

Automatically she switched off lights and motor, yanked on the hand-brake. She got out and slammed the door. Hearing, she went to the house, inside and up to her flat.

In the main room she turned on an electric fire and crouched in front of it, her face close to the bars. The heat bloomed. It took over from the diversion of travel. Jill thought only of her hot, tingling flesh.

Soon, however, the heat growing too strong, she had to sit back on her heels. Immediately she thought of Ben.

He was dead, not wounded. She was sure of that. There had been a finality in the slow collapse and in the scream.

But was it dream-true, or reality-true? Had she, in fact, imagined the whole thing?

Jill shuddered. The spasm was total, as thorough as the shake a dog gives itself on emerging from water. Her whole body was affected. After the shudder had passed, her hair continued dithering.

She felt strange. In her thought processes she was herself, but those thoughts were warped by dread. She wanted to run, and she wanted to curl up small. She wanted to sob harshly, and she wanted to chuckle at the absurdity of it all.

Had she murdered? Had she killed Ben?

"Ridiculous," Jill said. The word rang shrill and meaningless.

She got up and crossed to a sideboard. From one of its cupboards she took a glass and a half bottle of brandy. Noticing now her gloved hands, she stripped them and put the gloves in a drawer. She poured a small measure of alcohol, which she drank straight off.

Gratefully she coughed and spluttered. The brandy cauterised. She was sorry when, eyes moist, she found the strong effects fading. But she bustled in putting bottle and glass back in the cupboard.

Abruptly Jill hissed out a snicker. She followed it with a gasp of fear and shot both hands to her face in containment. She squeezed her cheeks, distorting her lips into ugly shapes. Only when she felt sure that no more snickers were due did she let her arms fall.

"I'm all right," she said. "I'm going to be fine. There's nothing wrong with . . ." But she couldn't finish. She couldn't face the last indignity.

The figure in the doorway had been made of paper, Jill told herself, not flesh and blood. The scream had been a noise, not a human voice. The car had been a Jaguar like a thousand others, not Ben's. And it was all a daydream away.

Jill smiled. It was a faint, sad smile and her eyes were distant.

Striding, she went around the flat switching on lights and drawing curtains. She finished up in the kitchen. After using four matches, three of which broke, she put flame under the kettle.

Jill knew, however, that tea was not the answer. In any case, she felt unequal to the chore of preparation. The dozen steps needed to reach the ready cup struck her now as immensely complex, like a journey abroad.

She turned the flame off. Still with her hand on the knob, she paused. She turned it. Gas whispered from the jets. She lowered her head and sniffed. Not bad, she thought, as she turned it off.

Lurching around fast, Jill left the kitchen and went to the door of the flat. She let herself out. The stairs she descended briskly. She went outside. As soon as she had passed through the garden gate, she started running.

Jill chased thought. She scattered the ranks of knowledge. She routed possibility. Nothing was in her mind as she went as fast as she could along street after street, taking any direction that presented itself.

Lights and movement filled her vision, her ears were busy sorting out the sounds of the night. There was comfort in the steady drubbing of her feet, a beat she could feel at the back of her head. She was light of heart.

Jill ran for an hour. She used every gait from fast jog to full-out racing. The last was the best but, unfortunately, could be maintained for only short periods.

Wherever she passed, Jill caused a nine-second wonder.

Drivers blew their horns, a drunk tried to grab her arm, youths called to know about the fire, couples stood aside to make way, a beat constable stared.

Exhaustion drew Jill to a walk, then a ragged amble, and at last a halt. She leaned against a wall, panting painfully. Her body started to droop—which reminded her.

She saw the figure in the hallway, heard the scream.

"A target," Jill gasped. "A noise."

Pushing away from the wall she went on at a slurred walk. Her body was slimy with sweat and she was shivering. She had a stitch. Her thighs and shoulders ached from running. It all helped.

Jill argued to herself that nothing had happened, that she had not been out of the flat, except now, for this walk. She was not the kind of fool who would go shooting in the dark.

"Imagination," Jill said, turning into Cheever Street. She entered the house softly and climbed to her door. With it closed behind her she stood and felt the silence.

Frightened anew, she went along to her bedroom. She looked in her wardrobe. The gun wasn't there. That fact she forced home by verbalising it: "The gun isn't here."

Of course it wasn't, she told herself. You dropped it on the gravel.

She ignored that.

The rifle was not there. The evening had been a daydream. The whole thing had been a daydream, from the first moment she had started to act oddly, getting in the Rolls-Royce. That hadn't really happened. She had not put a pound note in the charity box or complained of the tea being cold. She had not met Ben again in a pub, had not stolen a gun, had not done other strange things, had not gone on dates with Ben and practiced shooting. She had not gone out tonight and fired at a target in a doorway.

It was a daydream, or it was true; she was mistaken, or she had killed.

Jill didn't know which to work for, hope for. She went down the passage and into the kitchen. She turned on the gas and listened to the hiss.

Nodding, switching off, Jill left the kitchen. Her face was void of expression. She was like that inside. A cold, flat calm had come in place of the shifts between fear and ridicule.

She went into the bathroom. Her movements slow but sure, determined, she stripped and stepped into the shower. The water she let drum at full pressure on her head, rendering it a bowl of sound; nothing more.

When Jill was beginning to sway with tiredness, she got busy. She tended to her body first. Next she soaped and washed her hair, doing the chore with unusual thoroughness. After a final rinse, she dried herself and put on a robe.

In her bedroom, bent over, Jill spent some time rubbing her hair with a towel. The rough action joined defence forces with the blood pounding in her ears. She sat on the bed and fitted over her head the plastic cap of a hot-air dryer. She switched on. Again she was rendered thoughtless by noise.

Half an hour later, Jill was dressed in a trouser suit. It was her best, most recent outfit. Her shoes were new. She had donned what little jewellery she owned. Her hair was brushed out, dry except for stray ends. She had put on make-up with the same care she had taken during her whole toilette, as if she were preparing for an outing of import.

Jill had a final check in the mirror. She twisted and turned solemnly, looking from every angle, and finished with a survey of the front. She avoided her eyes.

Going out and along to the living room, she sat at a writing desk. She opened a pad and picked up a pen. Leaning forward, she poised the pen over the paper. She waited.

Jill sat thus for fifteen minutes. The right words stayed elusive, flickering somewhere at the back of her mind. Instead, she went interminably over the thoughts that had already raked her emotions.

She got up to go to the kitchen.

The telephone rang.

Crossing to it, Jill lifted the receiver. She said an involuntary, "Is that you, Ben?" She was not acting, even for herself. For the moment she had forgotten.

A male voice asked gravely, "Am I speaking to Miss Jillian Parr?"

"Oh," Jill said. "Yes." She had remembered. Her body went weak. Without surprise or interest she found herself sinking to the floor. She sagged to her knees, then to a sit on the carpet. Had she not put out her free hand as a stay, she would have fallen over sideways.

"Miss Parr," the man said, "my name's Wain. Inspector Wain of the Middlesex police."

"Police?"

"Yes. I'm sorry to disturb you, I know how late it is, but I wonder if I might come and see you at once?"

Jill asked, "What is it? What's wrong?" Now she was acting, for self and caller.

"I'd rather not discuss it over the telephone, if you don't mind. I can be with you in five minutes. I'm here in your locality, at the police station."

"I see," Jill said, curiously neat and prim.

"I'll be with you presently then, Miss Parr. Good-bye for now." The line clicked to silence.

Jill reached up and returned the receiver to its cradle. She had to take hold of the table edge to help herself upright. Standing was an effort. Her knees felt numb, as if iced.

Acting again, she lifted the receiver and dialled Ben's number. The call-signal rang. It went on ringing, a melancholy cry in duplicate. Ben was not there. Jill, however, didn't disconnect. She went on listening to the signal until a knock came on the flat door.

As she went through to the passage, Jill primped herself, touching hair and clothes and jewellery. She stopped to stare at herself in a mirror. She hardly knew that face.

Another knock sounded. Jill answered it.

There were two men. The one who introduced himself as Inspector Wain was about forty years old. He had a tall, slender body. His hair was long and lank. His thin face was unremarkable save for the fact that it had a mistake mouth—plump and babyish, pouting. His eyes were green, watchful, steady.

Inspector Wain wore a crumpled sports coat, as did the other man, who was cursorily introduced as a Detective Sergeant Brown, of the local police.

Jill took the men into the main room, where she faced them with, "Is it something to do with Ben? Mr. Armitage, that is."

Wain nodded. "Yes, miss."

"If he's had an accident, I'd like to know at once."

"We'll get to that in a minute, Miss Parr," the policeman said. Nor was his attitude giving anything away. "First I'd like to ask you a few questions."

"Very well."

Wain looked pointedly at the seating. Jill lowered herself onto a couch. "Please sit down." From the top of her mind she told herself that Ben had been in a slight traffic skirmish. She was empty calm.

The local man, obviously a mere observer, had taken a straight-backed chair by the wall. Inspector Wain had brought one forward. Sitting close, crossing his legs with an elegance out of atmosphere, the pout-mouthed man folded his arms and asked,

"Where were you all this evening, Miss Parr?"

"I? Where was *I?*"

"Yes. These are routine questions. Did you go out?"

"Why no," Jill said. Her voice was as toneless as her features were free of expression. "I stayed home all evening."

"Was anyone else here? Did anyone telephone?"

She shook her head. "I was alone. No calls. I did little jobs. Ironing, cleaning. I washed my hair." She touched a damp hank.

The policeman resettled the grip of his folded arms. It was a movement that seemed to imply satisfaction. He asked, "How well did you know the Farnsworths?"

Jill's emptiness was pierced. She experienced an emotion. It was surprise. She said, "Who?"

"Mr. and Mrs. Farnsworth. Harold and Valerie. Harry and Val to their friends, I understand. How well do you know them?"

"I don't. I mean, I've never heard of these people."

Inspector Wain raised his eyebrows. "Really?"

"Really," Jill said. "Oh, no. Wait. Farnsworth. That could be Ben's superior at the bank."

"That's right. You never met him, or his wife?"

"No, never."

"Then, of course, you've never been to their house."

"Obviously not, Inspector."

"That's rather odd," Wain said, "with you being engaged to Ben Armitage."

Jill was surprised again. "Engaged?"

"We understood that you were Mr. Armitage's fiancée. We assumed that you were his closest connexion, next of kin."

"Oh. Well. I see."

The policeman tilted his head as if interrogating a child. "You're not engaged?"

"Not really," Jill said. "Not exactly. I don't know."

Inspector Wain implied more satisfaction with his arms. He

let a long moment go by before asking his next question, "Do you own a car?"

"Yes, I do. Yes."

Wain got out an envelope and a stub of pencil. "If you could give me the make, year, colour and licence number, please, miss."

She told him. He made notes on the back of the envelope. After that he got up. So did the other man. So did Jill. She asked, "Is that all?"

"For the time being, yes," Wain said. "We'll be meeting again. The main purpose of this call was to let you know about Armitage."

"What's happened to him?"

"He's at Cranwell."

"Is he all right?" Jill asked, acting, and grateful that the policeman was acting with her.

Wain put away pencil and envelope. Patting his pockets he said, "I'm sorry to have to break this to you, Miss Parr. I hope it won't come as too great a shock."

"Tell me."

"Perhaps you should sit down again."

"Tell me."

Inspector Wain said, "Well, by tomorrow evening we will probably bring a charge against Armitage."

Jill wrinkled her face. "You'll bring a what?"

"A charge, miss. If nothing new comes up, Ben Armitage will be charged with murder."

Jill's face relaxed. She felt calm, dead calm. She said politely, "Would you repeat that, please."

Wain said, "Your boy friend or fiancé, Miss Parr, is suspected of having killed Valerie Farnsworth."

Jill stared. She lifted her chin. Slowly she moved over to the Inspector. For a while longer she stared on at him in silence. Then words came. She spoke them at a measured pace,

"I am going mad. Do you realise that I am losing my mind? I have suspected it for some time. I am going mad. Do you understand? Do you hear me?"

The policeman lifted his arms and began to spread them. When they were wide apart at shoulder height, he abruptly swung them together. His hands met in a loud clap.

Jill swayed. She lifted both hands to her cheeks. "What?"

"You were screaming," Wain said.

"Oh."

"Please sit down. Cry if you can."

She began to cry.

THREE

As Ben came to the surface of consciousness, he was smiling. Then he became aware of the grey beyond the slits of his near-open eyes. He opened them fully—and remembered.

The smile ebbed. It had belonged to his dream, which was one he had regularly, seeing himself walking along a beach hand in hand with Val. That golden scene had been replaced by this terrible reality.

It was early morning, he had been asleep under a coarse blanket but with all his clothes on, the dreary grey light came through a window that had heavy bars.

Ben closed his eyes again. He wanted to go back into the dream. He would have preferred to go back to yesterday. He didn't want to have to repeatedly work at accepting the unbelievable, that Val was dead. He wanted that to be a dream. And he wanted to get rid of this sensation in his chest; it was as if he had a cavity there with sore edges.

It isn't fair, he thought. Why me?

His throat began to ache, he felt tears coming. Every nerve and sinew urged him to roll over onto his face, and weep. Instead he jerked up and thrust the blanket aside. He sat on the edge of the bed.

Taking deep breaths to dispel emotion, he told himself that if he gave in he was lost. He had to fight. Sadness he could afford to show, but not grief. He had to keep Val out of his mind. Fortunately, he was well practiced in that.

Calmer, Ben looked at his watch. It told him seven o'clock.

He gazed around the small room that earlier he had been too sleep-sodden to notice. He had been concerned solely with fumbling his shoes off and getting under cover, out of sight, alone.

There was a single bed with an iron frame, a table with two chairs, a lavatory and a washbowl. The room was bare but not outright severe—its furniture painted blue, the bedding patterned, bright linoleum on the floor. Ben reminded himself that despite the window bars the place was a detention room, not a cell.

Which, he thought drably, in no way improved the situation. It was a matter of degree of confinement, a nicety of semantics. Phrase it or colour it as you like, he was still a prisoner.

But Ben was not overly worried. On that side of the affair, he was merely astonished. The whole thing was incredible. The fantasy had two prongs. One, that he was suspected of murder. Two, that Jill had actually followed his dress-rehearsal orders.

Ben mused that distance, patently, was not a factor in mind-control. He should have known that. Three miles, ten miles, even fifty, it made no difference once the rapport was established. Jill had obeyed his every thought. She had driven to the cottage, had knocked, had aimed at . . .

That cavity in Ben's chest, it started to burn. He switched his mind away from grief by giving careful attention to the putting on of his shoes. Next he washed. He was able to get satisfaction out of there being no hot water. Last he combed his hair.

In spite of being weary, Ben began to pace the room. It was a five-stride trip each way between window and door. He was unable to stop himself going over the events of last night, but saw them objectively, the by-stander.

Sitting in the armchair in the cottage parlour, Ben had been imagining himself at the Minstrel Boy, in the washroom after having greeted his guests. He was in one of the stalls, concentrating deeply, repeating over and over what Jill should do. From there, he had been snatched back to the parlour by a sharp cracking noise.

At once he recognised it as a gunshot. It was followed by another while he was slamming up to his feet. He was dazed by what seemed the incredible coincidence of such sounds happening at this exact moment, fitting with his thoughts.

But was it coincidence, a similarity of noises? The shots were still going on. It was a repetition he had come to know so well in recent days. The sounds were coming from outside, on the turnabout.

Ben got to the parlour door fast, yanked it open. The last shot had been fired. He stood in the doorframe and stared at Val. She was turning lazily toward him. Blood was coughing from several points on her chest. She wore a smile of restrained annoyance. Her eyes had no movement.

Ben screamed. He failed to catch Val as she fell. He whimpered at the ugly thud her head made on hitting the floor. He groaned when seeing that the blood was no longer spurting. Kneeling, he cradled Val in his arms.

Harry appeared. He came rushing from the direction of the bathroom along the hall. From then on, all was a confusion of soreness and action and disbelief.

Ben didn't know how long he sat there in the hall holding Val, or what he said, or what Harry said. He wasn't sure which of them had telephoned a doctor. The confusion grew as men began to arrive. He was given a brandy. There were questions, orders, movements in and out. More people kept on arriving. At one stage the parlour seemed to have twenty men present, uniformed and in mufti.

He was questioned by a sergeant, answered the same questions from a detective, and went through the whole exchange again with another plainclothesman. A constable came in carrying a rifle, there were men with cameras, a pompous doctor, medical people in white. Ben began to be frightened by the stupidity of it all.

That he was suspected of the killing didn't occur to Ben until much later, at a police station, when he was questioned yet again, now by an Inspector Wain. This served only to increase his disbelief.

The Inspector left. Ben was given tea and a sandwich, had his fingerprints taken, had the contents of his pockets examined. Last, he was asked to relinquish his belt and tie. He asked why. He was told it was so he wouldn't be able to hang himself.

After a tedious wait, Inspector Wain returned and once more the questions started. Ben stood it for half an hour. He protested that he was falling asleep. The Inspector showed him to a bed.

Now, pacing the detention room, Ben shook his head. There had been no reality whatever about the evening, and his own role as a murder suspect was ridiculous.

At least one thing had been explained, however: Val's presence downstairs. Harry had brought her down from the studio to watch a saucepan while he went to the bathroom.

Ben experienced a surge of hate for Harry Farnsworth. He walked rapidly, clenched fists held before him as if trying to pull a piece of string apart. His face became congested, eyes staring, lips open and wet.

The excess of emotion made him weak. He found himself stumbling. He forced himself away from the thoughts of his enemy by considering again the fluke of Val being downstairs at the wrong moment.

It, he mused, was that human element which he had always been wary of, which could spoil the finest, most detailed of plans. It could have happened just as well on Saturday night.

It wasn't his fault. The scheme was basically sound, decidedly clever. If Val hadn't been so willing, so kind, so . . .

Ben stopped the approaching memoir. He had to be strong. He was in danger. His mental best was needed. Last night he had managed well, despite being in shock—saying that Jill Parr was his fiancée, that had been a smart move. Last night he had done well, today he must do better.

Without ceremony the door was opened. A constable entered with a tray. He said, "Breakfast."

"Hearty?" Ben asked, cold. His wit was wasted. The constable merely nodded as he put the tray down. Back at the door he said, "When you've done, Inspector Wain's going to have another talk with you."

Alone, Ben sighed. Nor was he cheered on looking down at the bacon and eggs, tea and bread. He was too shattered for food. The ache in his empty stomach was cowed by that larger ache above.

Ben realised, however, that his not eating would make a bad impression, give the idea that worry was killing appetite.

Save for a crust of bread, he flushed all the food away down the lavatory. He was sitting at the table with the mug of tea when next the door opened.

Inspector Wain had dark smudges under his eyes, themselves red and heavy-lidded. This offered Ben a measure of pleasure. Also, it helped in cancelling the resentment he had felt previously toward the other man on account of his comparative youth in relation to his rank. What Ben didn't resent he could feel superior to.

"I see you ate well, Mr. Armitage."

"Not bad. Considering."

Wain sat on the edge of the bed. "Sleep well too?"

"Did my conscience bother me? No, it didn't. I slept."

"Then you should be in good form to answer questions."

Ben exaggerated a groan. "Surely we're not going to go through all that again."

"Not necessarily. Only if you want to make changes in that story of yours."

"No changes."

Wain nodded. He rubbed a hand over his face. "Tired. I was up late last night. I went to see your fiancée."

"Good."

"Except that Miss Jillian Parr doesn't seem so sure about being engaged to you."

Ben shrugged. "It wasn't official. We didn't put an item in the paper or buy a ring. It was simply an understood thing. To me, anyway."

"Sure you don't want to change your story?"

A bluff, Ben thought. "Quite sure, thanks."

With another nod the Inspector said, "So you still deny that a special relationship existed between you and Mrs. Farnsworth?"

"I do."

"Fine. Then let me tell you this. Last night, while holding the deceased in your arms, you said, several times, 'I love you.'"

Ben looked down to carefully move his tea mug out of the way. "I know I did," he lied, looking up. "It was true. I did love Val, and Harry. They're the only friends I have in the world."

The Inspector twitched his thick lips. "You also said, several times, 'I didn't mean it.'"

This one took a little longer. Ben nodded slowly for many seconds before saying, "Yes. I'm glad I told her that. But I'm afraid it was too late."

"Meaning?"

"I was referring to something I'd said about her work, her art. It wasn't flattering. In fact, she was hurt."

"Mr. Farnsworth didn't mention that."

"I'd be surprised if he knew, if, in fact, Val had told him. One doesn't repeat insults. Where is Harry, by the way? Is he all right?"

"He's at the home of friends, under sedation now. Before that, we had a couple of long talks."

"Poor Harry. This is going to break him. They were devoted to each other."

"Oh?" the Inspector said. He rubbed his face again. "Mr. Armitage, about two weeks ago, you stopped Harry Farnsworth near here in his car. Remember that?"

Careful, Ben thought. He nodded. "Yes."

"According to Farnsworth, you were agitated. You said you had made a mistake, flagged down the wrong car. You said you had a date there with a woman."

Ben shook his head. "That was Harry's assumption—the woman bit. Agitated? Yes, I suppose I was."

"Why, Mr. Armitage?"

This one was easy now. "Because what I'd planned to do was illegal. I was nervous. As it happens, the deal didn't come off, and I'm glad. I shan't bother again."

"Would you explain, please."

"Marijuana," Ben said. "I've often thought it would be interesting to try the stuff. A man I met in a pub one night, he offered to sell me some. He was supposed to meet me at that junction. He didn't show."

Wain folded his arms in time with a long, slow nod. "Very neat. I congratulate you. The man, of course, is unknown to you, and wouldn't come forward to corroborate your story."

"It's true that I don't know him. Corroboration, yes, I imagine you're right, if he's a dealer in drugs."

Wain asked, "Shall I tell you what you were really doing at the deserted junction?"

"Feel free."

"It's very simple. You were waiting for Valerie Farnsworth. There was no mistake about the car. It was the family Rover, all right. But the husband was in it, not the wife. There'd been a hitch."

Ben felt dreary at how neatly it fitted. He asked, "Is that what Harry thinks?"

"He doesn't think anything. He was just telling us. He doesn't want to believe that his wife was having a love affair, with you or anyone else."

"Then why did he tell you about that night?"

"There were those things you said in the hall. Also, earlier, you had asked about the gate to the property being open, as if you were concerned that someone might come and, perhaps, interrupt what you had in mind."

"Hindsight. A casual remark, a bit of idle chat, can take on all kinds of sinister implications."

"And, of course," Wain said, "there are the letters. Harry Farnsworth found them at the cottage last night."

Ben's leg muscles tightened. "What letters?"

"Love letters, Mr. Armitage. Written by you to the deceased. As the saying goes, hot stuff."

Ben looked down at the hands he had pressed between his thighs. This was getting more difficult and unbelievable by the minute. He could feel damp in his armpits. In his throat, a fluttery sensation had come into being. It was stronger than that sore-edged cavity in his chest.

He said, "I see."

"That makes you think, eh?"

"It moves me. I didn't know that Val had kept those letters."

Wain asked, "Do you still deny that you were having an affair with Valerie Farnsworth?"

Ben looked up. "Oh, yes. There was no affair. I had a crush on Val at one time. Years ago. I wrote her. It didn't even get

as far as the kissing stage. She was devoted to her husband."
He was able to produce a sad smile. "How sweet though that
she kept my letters."

"Neat again," Wain said coldly. "But weak. You know, of
course, that the letters are undated. Even so, I think our ex-
perts should be able to say how old they are."

All Ben's weariness seemed to press on him at once. He
said, sagging, "Look. You're wasting your time. I did not kill
Val. All the time you waste trying to tie me to the murder,
that's an advantage to the real killer."

"We're not standing still. We're checking all leads. But it's
routine. If you didn't kill her, who did?"

"There are several possibilities. A homicidal maniac. Or, as
you seem to favour the sex angle, a wife who suspected her
husband of having an affair with Val. For all anyone knows,
Harry could have been having an affair."

Wain said, "I prefer my own theory. The sex angle is
Valerie Farnsworth and Benjamin Armitage."

Ben looked at the policeman with open dislike. "So if we
were having an affair, why did I kill her?"

"She'd had enough of you," Wain said. "She'd been wanting
to quit for some time. But not you. There's an unmistakable
pleading tone in those letters of yours. She wanted out, and
you wouldn't accept it."

"Therefore I murdered her in cold blood."

"All murder is cold-blooded, Mr. Armitage."

"Hell," Ben said wearily, "why don't you go away."

Wain yawned. He didn't turn his face aside, and he made
no attempt to cover his mouth. This sent a charge of fury
through Ben. He stood up. One leg was trembling. He said,

"I bet you like your job."

"What does that mean?"

"That you're probably a class-A bastard."

"I see," Wain said blandly.

Ben sneered, "One of those hen-pecked slobs who always go for the jobs that'll give 'em a slice of power—cop, prison warder, things like that."

"Go on, Armitage."

Ben did go on, despite knowing that losing his temper could be exactly what Wain wanted. He was too angry to care. The anger was a cover for fear. Mention of the letters being found had reminded Ben of an item he had in his bedroom, one he had planned to get rid of today. It was the box, now empty, that had contained the .22 bullets. It was clearly marked as to contents. If the police got a search warrant . . .

"You don't give a damn if I'm guilty or not," Ben snapped. "What you do love is being able to say whatever you like to a man and get away with it. Outside your job, you'd tremble at the idea of offending a cripple dwarf. Here you're brave, you're big, you're a tough guy. You think you're safe."

Ben leaned forward and put his fists on the table. "Don't be too sure. I have my limits. Any more insults from you and I'll belt you in your rotten baby mouth."

Wain got up. He smiled as he went past to the door, where he said, "Spoken like a true man of violence."

Jill awoke at ten. Jets of sunshine were shooting in around the curtains like slivers of rainbow. Lying still, she looked at the familiar room and thought of how normal she felt. Or near to normal.

There was a continuing buzz in her head. It was not an ache exactly, more like a numbness, as though her brain were fatigued from a great deal of cogitation. It had been the same in sleep, Jill realised. After a series of pleasant dreams—one was watching Ben and someone she knew must be his sister walking along a beach—there had been no more pictures, only sensations; she had felt confined and agitated and despondent.

Jill sat up in bed. She said, "Ben. He's alive. He's alive and unhurt."

That was what she had to cling to. It was the keystone to her safety and sanity. Although it didn't explain everything, it did mean that in some degree she was mistaken about last night.

A wary expression came into Jill's eyes. It had occurred to her that she could not even be sure of the visit here of the two policemen.

She got quickly out of bed and went through to the main room. Casting about, she saw an ash tray, stalked to it and found there only butts with the name of her own brand, and all bearing lipstick. Turning, however, she saw evidence on a side table: a calling card bearing a name and a telephone number.

Smiling with uncertainty, a flicker like the approach to tears, Jill remembered gratefully the attitude of Inspector Wain. He had seemed to accept her outburst as natural. He had brought water, asked repeatedly if she needed a doctor or a friend's company, talked soothingly, and had not left until she had insisted she was recovered.

In the kitchen Jill put a light under the kettle. She didn't think about the gas. The sun was shining and for the moment she felt herself, whole and healthy. And Ben was alive. These factors weakened those others that should be making her ill and which she would refuse to dwell on until she'd had her tea; even the crazy one about Ben.

Inspector Wain had explained quietly that Ben was suspected of having been involved romantically with Valerie Farnsworth. The affair had gone sour, police theory went, and Ben had killed his mistress, shooting her from out on the gravel and dropping the gun there.

Jill forgot about tea as it came to her, with a rush, that all could be explained by the police theory. She *had* stayed home last night. She'd sat around and read and passed an uneventful evening—until the detectives had come. She had been upset at their news of Ben's arrest, so upset that she had dreamt the complete scene as Wain had described it, except that she herself was the protagonist. That had been because her subconscious believed in Ben's innocence.

Jill mulled this over excitedly while the kettle boiled and she made tea. She also remembered that the gun used in the murder was called a two-two, whereas the rifle here—if one ever had been here—was a three-o-three.

"A dream," Jill said aloud. She hugged herself through the thin nightgown. "I dreamt it all."

With a tight, wide smile she poured tea while dismissing swiftly in one section of her mind what she had said to Inspector Wain. She was not going mad. Nor had she done any of those oddities. They were dreams or imaginings.

"But I must get out of the habit of talking to myself inside," she said. She drained her cup and poured out another. About to drink, she paused as the telephone rang.

"Now what? Bad news? No, there couldn't be any worse than what is. It might be Ben to say they've let him go." Jill put down her cup.

In the main room she lifted the receiver, gave her number. A man's voice asked, "Am I addressing Miss Jill Parr?"

"Yes. Who is it, please?"

"Good morning. My name's Cartwright. I'm with the *Daily Star* and I'd like to ask—"

Jill slammed the receiver down. Hurrying to her bedroom she began to dress. She had to get out of the house as quickly as possible. There were reporters to avoid. Also, there was Ben to see. Inspector Wain had said she could visit Ben this morning, and had warned that she might be pestered by the press.

Jill's smile became less fixed, warmer, as she recalled that not only had Ben asked that she be informed of his situation, not only had he listed her as his next of kin, but he had referred to her as his fiancée.

Jill blushed. She felt happy and curiously free. Which made her want to cry.

That ended as the telephone shrilled again. Ignoring it, Jill went on with her dressing. She was putting on the trouser suit she had worn last night while sitting around all evening waiting for Ben to call.

Jill wondered about the craziness of Ben's position. But she was unable to worry. She felt sure he would never be charged with murder. Jill believed in the ultimate triumph of judicial truth. The police would find the real killer in the end.

She dropped the scarf she had been about to put on. Bustling, she left the room and went out of the flat. The telephone was still ringing. Downstairs she opened the front door cautiously, peering through the two-inch crack.

With relief she saw not a fraction of the scene that her expectations had been building: dozens of predatory reporters, all snatching at her and snarling questions and popping flashbulbs in her face. The street was deserted.

As Jill made to open the door wider and go out, however, she saw a car draw to a stop nearby. There were two men in the front, strangers. She thought they could be press, or police, or no one in particular. She didn't want to find out.

Jill closed the door and went to the rear of the house. She let herself out and hurried across the garden. Climbing a low fence, she had no qualms about using the next property, it was a short cut she had taken before.

Jill got a peculiar gratification from this act of sneaking away. It was as if she were making a prankish escape. As in her sleep, the faint buzz in her head was like the feeling caused by confinement.

Out on a road that ran parallel with Cheever Street, Jill set off walking. Ten minutes later she stopped a vacant taxi.

Cranwell was out of metre range, the cabbie said. The price he quoted to drive her there made Jill swallow.

Enjoying the worry of expense, she agreed and got in. During the drive she thought about dreams, both the day and night variety, and marvelled at how realistic they could be.

Cranwell, a county town, was a collection of narrow streets, each like a conveyor belt slowly carrying vehicles bumper to bumper. Walking, Jill had no need to ask. Signs pointed the way to library, public conveniences, post office, police station.

The last was all black brickwork and Gothic eaves. It was also the centre of attraction for half a dozen men whose slouch and outsize cameras gave their profession away. Jill could understand the interest of the press. It wasn't every day that a bank official was suspected of murder.

Acting nonchalance, Jill crossed the road, passed between the men and went inside the building. In an office that smelt of disinfectant, she asked the sole occupant, a uniformed officer, if she could please see Mr. Armitage. She gave her name.

His eyebrows raised with interest, his lips hard together as though to prevent himself asking questions, the policeman came from behind the counter and led Jill along a passage.

Turning a corner, they met Inspector Wain. He stopped and nodded. He looked exhausted, Jill thought. She said, "Hello."

"Good morning, Miss Parr. Feeling better?"

"Fine, thanks. Sorry about last night."

"Perfectly understandable."

Jill asked, "You haven't let Ben go, then?"

"I'm afraid not," Wain said, solemn. "Little things keep turning up. I told him the latest just now. He has an explanation, of course."

"Oh, I'm sure he has, Inspector. Ben's innocent."

As if she had not spoken, Wain said, "I pointed out that the loan he claims to have wanted to discuss had already been cleared. Farnsworth says so. There were no problems. Armitage says he mis-read the papers."

"Well, there you are."

"It doesn't jell, Miss Parr. The whole thing smells."

Jill, edging past, said a feeble, "It's all nonsense."

Inspector Wain asked, "If he didn't do it, who did?"

"I haven't the vaguest idea," she said sharply. "Excuse me."

Ben was sprawled on the bed. He had been like that, had not bothered to get up, when Wain had come in with his latest, and weakest, development.

Now, as the door opened, Ben got quickly to his feet on seeing Jill. He went toward her and said, "How wonderful to see you." He added, for the benefit of the policeman who was closing the door, "Darling."

They embraced. Easing back, Ben kissed her lightly on the lips. He said, "It was good of you to come and see me."

While Jill was protesting that it was nothing of the kind, and while she was asking how he felt, had he slept well and been given something to eat, Ben was looking at her closely.

She had signs of tension and shock, he saw. Her face possessed little in the way of animation. She stood meekly with hands clasped. Her eyes were dull. There was a mechanical tone and rhythm to her voice.

He wondered what she thought of it all. Her appearance was hardly due to distress at the fact of his threatened arrest—though that was possible, since she did have a case on him.

But no, Ben mused, obviously it was more than that. She was holding on. There was fear in her stance, dread in her eyes, worry of collapse in the way her hands clung to one another.

Imagination, Ben thought. She was trying to pass what had happened last night off as something she had imagined, the way she'd been ordered to do with the beer glass and his absences from the flat. Let her try.

After seeing Jill into a chair at the table, Ben sat at the other side. He said, "At least they've allowed us to be alone together."

"Yes."

"I'm technically free, of course. If I'm charged it'll be different. This is called assisting the police, if you please."

"But, Ben," Jill said. "What evidence have they got to make a charge with?"

"As far as I can see, none. Flimsy bits of the circumstantial type. Really, Jill, I'm not frantic about this predicament. You mustn't be either."

"Inspector Wain seems so confident."

"He's a hick trying to be smart," Ben said. He touched her shoulder. "I didn't do it, you know."

"Of course you didn't."

"You do believe that, don't you, Jill?"

"I do," she said. She might have been agreeing that it was a chilly day. "You're no killer."

"Apart from that, there's no point, no motive. Why on earth should I want to shoot Val? No, the answer's obvious."

"Yes?"

He nodded. "It was some lunatic."

Jill flinched. She said, as if in a hurry to get the words out, "There must be something I can do to help. A lawyer. I could contact one for you."

"They told me I could do that, last night. I said that as long as they let you know where I was, that would do. I said that since I was innocent I had no use for a lawyer."

"That must have scored in your favour."

"I think so."

Jill was fumbling in her pocket for cigarettes. Letting her go on doing that, Ben got up and took a turn at pacing. He

realised he was on delicate ground with Jill Parr and her in-
volvement. What he had to do was implicate her in the murder
but keep himself completely out of it. After all, he was innocent.

He stopped by the door and looked at his visitor. She had a
cigarette going now, but it was resting in her fingers. Faced the
other way, she seemed to be staring out of the window.

Ben felt a sudden, vicious return of that agonised condition
in his chest as he thought of Val, his beautiful Val, dead and
mutilated, a hulk, while this foolish and plain creature sat here
alive and healthy.

Jill stirred. Ben, after a moment's struggle with the balance
of his emotions, managed to turn his feelings to pure hatred,
lessening the pain. Jill shivered.

She glanced around. "What?"

To hide his face he swiftly rubbed a hand over it. He mumbled, "Mmm?"

"I thought you said something."

Ben went back to the table and sat. "Jill," he said, "my
problem is that I have to get the police to believe that I am not
the one they want. More accurately, I have to get them working in the right direction."

"Yes."

"Now how can I make them accept that someone else did
this murder?"

She was looking at him blankly. "I don't know."

Neither do I, he thought. Not yet. But there'll be an easy
answer. It only needs time and brains. Time. That's been an
important factor all the way along.

Jill asked, "What time is it, please?"

"Mm? Oh, it's nearly noon. Why?"

"I don't know," she said. "Nothing."

Ben swallowed a sigh. He shuffled closer, elbows on the
table. "Your gun," he said.

The cigarette fell from Jill's fingers and rolled across the wood. Her face didn't change expression but she brought her hands together in a tight clasp.

Ben retrieved the cigarette and tossed it into the lavatory. Covering Jill's hands with his, he asked, "Did you tell Inspector Wain that you had a rifle?"

Jill eased back slightly, a fraction, at the same time turning her head to the side without removing her gaze from his face. She repeated, "A rifle?"

Ben squeezed her hands. "A rifle, yes. You had a gun in your wardrobe. Remember?"

"In my wardrobe?"

"Yes. Your father left it there, you told me."

She was still looking at him obliquely. She said, "I've been so absent-minded lately."

"I didn't know that, Jill."

"I have. I forget things and I imagine things."

"It was a rifle," Ben said gently, kindly. "You showed it to me. You told me you had been out in the country with it, practicing. You told me you were a fairly good shot."

Fifteen seconds went by in silence. Ben looked directly at Jill, she looked at him with her head turned away. At last she said, "There's no rifle in my wardrobe."

"It isn't important. But it would be better if you didn't say anything about a gun to Wain. Okay? He's got a nasty little mind, that one. Okay?"

She nodded. "Okay."

"The rifle you had was called a two-two."

"I see."

Ben released her hands, clasped his own. He said, "Talking of the Inspector, I didn't mention to him that you had met Val."

"Val?"

"Valerie Farnsworth. The woman who was shot last night.

She was young and beautiful. You were not jealous of her. It was a tragedy that she should have been killed."

"I met her?" Jill asked.

"Yes. In the foyer at the movies once. Another time in a pub. Yes, you met Val."

"I've—I've met a lot of people."

"Of course you have, Jill," Ben said. His tone was forgiving. "She was a wonderful person. But you weren't jealous, not in the least. You liked her."

"Yes," Jill said. It wasn't an affirmative; it was merely a word. She turned her face to the front but looked down at the table.

"Did Inspector Wain tell you that he thinks I was having an affair with Val?"

"Yes."

Ben said, "I hope you didn't believe that."

"No, I didn't."

"Positive?"

"Yes."

"Good girl. Be sure to tell Wain that when you see him next. Say you don't believe for a moment that we were having an affair. Be quite firm about it. Make sure he understands you."

"All right."

"He's got it in his nasty little mind . . ." Ben began, and let the rest of the sentence die away.

Looking at Jill he leaned back and slowly, slowly put his clasped hands behind his head. Every muscle in arms, back and neck was tight. Under the circumstances, that was about as far as he could go in celebration. It wouldn't have done to jump up and laugh.

Ben had found the answer. He held a smile off his face by making a grimace as he broke his grip and stretched his arms high. He said, "God, I'm tired."

"Poor Ben."

"I must get some sleep," he said, rising. "I know you won't mind if I ask you to excuse me."

One minute later, Jill had gone and Ben, sitting, was putting his hands to his temples.

Jill came out onto the street from the police station. The abrupt brightness here increased her dazedness. She felt lost, childish. Underlying that was an emotion that Jill failed to recognise. It was disappointment. Always before in Ben's presence she had been assured, had been able to realise that she had been day-dreaming. Now that was reversed.

A man appeared in front of her. He had an insolent grin. He asked, "You haven't been in there to see Ben Armitage, have you, sweetheart?"

Jill shook her head gently, detoured the man, kept on moving. She walked slowly. Her surroundings were unfamiliar. She was shocked and afraid, and she couldn't remember where she had left the Hillman.

Confess.

The word came into Jill's mind as she was crossing the street. On the other side she had seen a sign indicating that down an alley there was the municipal car park. At the entry of the word she stopped dead. She was in the centre of the roadway.

A truck racketed to a shuddery halt. Its siren blasted. From the other side of her came a squeal of brakes that set off a chain of such squeals, each fainter than the last as they came from farther along the street.

Jill looked around, turning from radiator to radiator. Beyond them, through windshields, were angry faces and gesticulating hands. The truck siren blasted again. Jill looked at the driver questioningly for a moment before moving on.

She reached the kerb. There she recalled that she had come

here to Cranwell by taxi. Passing the alley, she went toward an approaching woman. She would ask about buses.

Confess.

The word came when the woman, smiling politely, had paused in answer to Jill's lifted hand and murmured, "Excuse me."

"Yes? Can I help you?"

The woman's smile turned to a gape as Jill let her hand fall and walked on.

Jill told herself quietly, dully, that the impulse was only to be expected. People who had vivid imaginations often didn't know where fiction ended and reality began. They were troubled by imitation guilts.

Jill had drawn level with a snack bar. Into its plastic and chrome marquee were set loudspeakers, mesh faces that were blaring a pop tune, an hysteria for drums and guitar.

Jill dawdled to a stop under the marquee. She was directly below a speaker. Its offering she absorbed eagerly, totally, filling her mind with each twang and thud, whine and crash. She was indifferent to the fact of being jostled, unaware of the stares from the curious.

The tune ended. Jill tightened her jaw. She relaxed it again when another musical panic started. She stayed on under the booming speaker. She was a peaceful nothing.

Tune followed tune. Ten had been played and Jill was still listening, feeding on the noise. She would have gone on doing so, but her full distraction was interrupted by recognition.

Coming along the street toward her was Inspector Wain. He was with a police constable. The pair were talking busily. Jill moved on, went to the snack bar entrance and slipped inside.

It was a large place with a new smell, like a glue factory. Because she was trying to be interested, struggling for distraction, Jill noticed her surroundings. There were twenty-odd tables and a counter and a juke box that belonged in outer space.

Confess.

Jill walked quickly to the counter. She stood there with other customers, some swinging lazily on stools. The music was less strident inside. Jill moved along until she was at the end where two youths were washing dishes in a slipshodly fast clatter.

At the other side of the counter, a girl uptilted her face for an order. Jill said, "Tea and a sweet roll, please."

The girl nodded. Jill went on, "I didn't have breakfast this morning. I couldn't eat. But you have to eat. It's best to. You know."

The girl had gone. Jill told herself that she would laugh about this daydream later. She was tempted to laugh now. There was a bubble like humour deep in her windpipe. It was climbing. It stopped as the waitress came back.

Confess.

Jill paid, added a large tip and said, "I'm being naughty today. Extravagant. I shouldn't really tell anyone this, but I took a taxi all the way here from town."

"Yes," the girl said. Her smile was strained. She glanced back twice while moving away.

Jill sipped her tea. It was weak but acceptable. In picking up her sweet roll, Jill glanced along the counter. Leaning there was Inspector Wain. He was still deep in conversation with the constable.

Jill turned to hide her face. Lifting the cup and plate, she moved off. She went to a far table, near the window, and sat there with her back to the counter.

Confess.

Jill closed her eyes. She was filled with a longing to be home. She wanted to be in bed, or washing clothes, or loung-

ing around in her old housecoat, or making a really good
strong cup of tea.

"May I join you, Miss Parr?"

Jill jerked her eyes open and her head up. Standing beside
the table, holding a coffee mug, was Inspector Wain. Jill had to
work to get out,

"If I'm going to be followed . . ."

"Oh, come now," the detective said. "There's no question of
that. I'll go to another table, if you like."

Jill felt a pang of regret for her attitude, which apology she
tried to show in her features. The man had been decent to her
last night. She said, "I'm sorry."

"May I sit here?"

"Yes."

Inspector Wain lowered himself into the chair across from
her. He asked, "Feeling better for seeing your boy friend?"

Jill's answer was to lift one shoulder and say, "This is all
very trying."

"Of course, Miss Parr."

"My nerves. They're ragged."

The Inspector said, "That's understandable." He sipped
from his mug. Jill sat limply and watched him. She made no
move to taste her snack.

Wain put the mug down, and Jill said, "Confess."

As the detective blinked, Jill started. She said a breath-
spaced, "Ben. Ben and I. We're hoping. The killer. He'll come
forward. Give himself up. Confess. We're hoping that. He
might come forward and confess."

"It sometimes happens, yes."

"I know it does. That's why I told you."

"But generally, the confession is from a crank, someone
who knows about the murder only because he has read of it in
the newspapers."

"I must be on my way," Jill said. She made no effort to move. Fear seemed to have drained her energy.

"Miss Parr," the Inspector said, his voice taking on a more confidential tone. "I must tell you that the case against Armitage is very strong."

"He didn't do it."

"Would you like me to tell you what we've got, especially the evidence pointing to an affair with the deceased?"

Jill shook her head. It occurred to her that there was some statement she ought to make in respect of the alleged love affair. She couldn't recall what.

Inspector Wain put a cigarette in his bulbous lips and flicked on a lighter. Puffing smoke, he said, "I've just come from a call on Mr. Farnsworth. I mentioned your name."

"I don't know him."

"So he said. But he told me that he thought your hobby, Miss Parr, was the occult."

"Occult?" she said. She felt worse for not knowing what he was talking about.

"You and Armitage met at a meeting of a psychical research organization."

"Oh, yes. My first time there. And last."

"It's not your hobby?"

"No. Does it matter?"

The policeman shrugged.

Confess.

"I really must be going," Jill said faintly. This time she was able to push herself up from the chair.

Inspector Wain also rose. "Very well, Miss Parr," he said. "But look. You may be interested in knowing what we propose to do this afternoon."

"What?"

"We're going to take the suspect out to the Farnsworth place. The cottage, as they call it."

Jill, wanting to move away, asked, "Why?"

Wain said, "We want Armitage to re-enact his movements of when he was there last night. And it came to me now that you might care to come along."

"No," she said quickly.

"You do have the right to refuse, of course."

She said, "There's no reason why I should refuse. Yes, I'll go along."

"Fine. If you could meet me at the police station later, say four o'clock?"

"Yes. I must be going now."

"You haven't touched your tea or roll, Miss Parr."

"No," she said. "Good-bye."

"Until four."

Jill got to the door and outside. She hurried away.

One hour later, Jill was approaching Cheever Street. All the way in on the bus's roundabout journey, she had fought that strange urge, that word, by inventing a teenage boy who confesses to the police, telling a tale of attempted burglary and panic shooting. Although she went over this repeatedly, she was unable to make it seem as real as her earlier daydream.

Hot, sweating, Jill turned off before reaching her own street and went the back way. "Confess," she said, in time with the word in her head. The word began to come again but she stopped it by briskly naming aloud the flowers she passed.

Home was near. Jill climbed the fence between properties. Crossing the lawn, she saw that her attention was being flagged by Mrs. Parkinson. The downstairs neighbour agitated in her window like a carnival grotesque. Jill hurried on and stopped by the wall, looking up.

Mrs. Parkinson raised the window and thrust her head out. Her eyes were glistening. "I saw it in the newspaper," she said in a loud whisper. "How terrible. But I didn't know it was anything to do with you, dear. Not until that policeman in plain clothes came to see me."

"Inspector Wain."

"That's it. He went up to see Miss Kelly too. And there's been reporters at the front all morning. Gone now. They tried to talk to me. I gave 'em the edge of my tongue, let me tell you."

"What did Inspector Wain want?"

"He wanted to know if I'd seen or heard you yesterday at about eight o'clock. I said I had. Heard you. I did, didn't I? I heard you moving around."

"Yes."

"Of course I did."

Confess.

Jill said, "Ben didn't do it."

"I should think not. How ridiculous. As if you'd go out with a young man who'd do something like that."

Jill moved away. "Thank you. I must get inside. Thank you."

Confess.

She hurried upstairs to her flat, where she went straight into the bathroom. The word came twice during the brief time it took her to strip and get under the shower. She turned the cold tap to half jet. The water drummed onto the crown of her head.

Her mind became blank, numb. She thought of nothing as she stared down at the twin streams of water running from her breasts like cartoon tears.

Confess.

Jill switched the tap over to full jet. The word came again. She began to sing. And the word came again. She turned off the water and got out of the shower. The word was waiting. She rubbed herself furiously with a towel while speaking aloud the alphabet backwards.

Confess.

Nothing seemed to hinder it. It was petulantly persistent, like a spoiled child saying, "I will, I will." It had become as frequent and regular as a metronome.

The word came while she viciously combed out her wet hair, and while she dressed in frock and sandals, and while she ran into the main room to put on her record player. She turned the volume up to high and sat with her face to the speaker.

Confess.

The urge to obey was so strong it was almost a pain. Ignoring it was like fighting against the natural in favour of the perverse or the evil.

Jill started screaming.

She choked herself off, clicked the music into silence, got up and strode to the door. Out of her flat she went upstairs. The door there had its key in the lock, as always. Jill went in.

Miss Kelly was sitting in a rocking chair, knitting. In her sixties, she had white hair and a brown face. Her expression was sad, like an old nun who wonders. She wore a coverall. At Jill's entrance she looked around with a smile.

"How nice," she said. Her voice had a hard edge. "And how are you, my dear?"

Jill nodded. "Fine."

"There was a man here to see me about you."

Confess.

Jill went to a window seat. She sat there looking out at the sky. Without preamble she said, "I took the gun and went out to the car. Please listen carefully. I put the rifle on the back seat and set off. I knew the route well. Soon I was out in the country."

Jill talked faster and raised her voice. There was such marvellous release in getting it all out. She felt better by the second. She even gestured to illustrate points and acts. She knew that everything she said was a lie, but that didn't matter. She was ridding herself of it.

She described the shots, the falling body, the scream, her retreat and escape.

Empty, mind at peace, the urge gone, Jill turned to look at the white-haired woman. At the movement, Miss Kelly blinked. She put down her knitting and took a small box from the pocket of her coverall. Fiddling with the volume on the deaf-aid microphone, she asked, "What was that, dear?"

The sergeant opened the door and stood aside. He said, "This way, sir."

As Ben went past and stepped outside into a cobblestoned yard, he told himself, See, they're still saying sir. They're still being polite.

This reminder was not to boost a flagging morale, an emotional straw to clutch at. Ben was mentally cheerful. His grief, that was another matter, he had realised in the past hours. It would be unchanged for a long time to come—might never change at all.

The yard behind the police station held a patrol car, a constable waiting at its wheel; Ben's Jaguar looking dusty and forlorn; a Black Maria that gave off a smell of stale beer and vomit.

When past the van, Ben stopped to take deep breaths of the air, which, after almost twenty hours in one small room, was as refreshing as a sea breeze to a miner.

Ben smiled, both at the air and the sense of freedom, then, catching sight of his reflection in a window of the Jaguar, he smiled at himself. He was neat and combed. He had shaved with a borrowed electric razor. He was wearing his tie, which had been returned along with his belt. He had lunched thoroughly on soup and a meat course and dessert, plain but plentiful.

Ben had made a total recovery from his previous depression, that relating to his predicament. The return to confidence had come with his idea of putting into Jill's head the desire to confess to the murder.

So pleased had Ben been with this that he had been able to work at it only intermittently. Also there had been interruptions. Finally, however, he had settled to profound concentration.

It had worked. Ben knew that. He had known the moment it started to happen. Jill had confessed. What made him certain of it he would not have been able to say. It had been something in his own mind, a sort of release. It was vaguely like having a shout continually thrown back by echo, and then having the echo cease.

Ben drew another deep breath. Jill had confessed, he thought in quiet triumph. It was now only a matter of time, short time, perhaps minutes, until he was given the news, followed by abject apologies from the hick police force. The news should have come earlier. About three hours had passed since Jill had talked. But, of course, there was red tape to be dealt with.

The sergeant appeared from behind at Ben's side. He gestured toward the waiting patrol car. "If you're ready, sir."

Ben asked, "Sure you don't want to handcuff me?"

The policeman shrugged. He went on, over to the car, where he opened the back door. Ben joined him at a stroll. He was on the point of getting in, bending, when he heard a thud. He looked around. Inspector Wain was crossing the yard from the other side.

Straightening again, Ben called, "Well?"

The Inspector changed course. "Well what?"

"Any—um—developments?"

"As a matter of fact, yes," Wain said. Stopping by the back

of the car, he lifted one foot and put it on the bumper. He looked more tired than ever.

Smiling inside, Ben asked, "Which development is . . . ?"

"You seem very sure that it's in your favour."

"Since I'm innocent, naturally I'm sure. And are we still going to go through with this re-enactment farce at the cottage?"

Nodding, the Inspector looked at his wristwatch. "Miss Parr should be waiting for me inside or out front. She's agreed to go with us."

Ben slanted his head with interest. "Indeed."

"We have no policewomen here. I thought it would be an idea to have Miss Parr play the part of the deceased in this."

"What about the husband of the deceased? You know, that dear old friend of mine who's been so busily trying to put the finger on me."

"I'll play Mr. Farnsworth," Wain said. "Which reminds me, he told me something about Miss Parr."

His acting nicely understated, Ben squared his shoulders to say, "If Harry told you that Jill and Val knew each other, he's lying. They never met."

"I believe that has been mentioned."

"Actually, they were due to meet tonight. I'd planned a get-together for several friends, to introduce Jill and announce our engagement. It was to be at the Minstrel Boy."

"I see."

Ben smiled. "Come to think of it, you can check on that. I'll give you the names of the other guests. I'd forgotten all about it."

The Inspector, Ben thought, looked depressed. Also his voice was dull as he said, "Later. One thing at a time."

"Ask Harry as well."

"Look. Farnsworth told me that you and Miss Parr were interested in the occult. Are you?"

Ben held his smile with difficulty. This could be tricky. He said, "Because we met at that freaky association in Hampstead? That's rich. We had a good giggle and left. Ask Jill."

Ben was relieved when the policeman again looked depressed, rubbing a hand over his pouty lips, and pleasantly surprised when he asked,

"Is Jill Parr very fond of you, would you say?"

Coolly, "That, friend, is none of your damn business."

"All right. But the gun is. We're checking on that."

"Good. Glad to hear you're not idle."

Wain smiled lazily. "It's possible you're not aware that every gun has a serial number, just like a car engine."

"Of course I know."

"Within the next few hours the manufacturer of the rifle will tell us which shop handled it, and then the shop will tell us who bought it—recently, if my guess is right."

"Fine. That'll let me out."

"Who bought it if not you?"

Ben suggested, "Santa Claus?" He was pleased with himself. It was his turn to do the needling. And it was good that he had lost that foolish panic. Innocent people did not get found guilty, which fact, his believing that, must show in his face even without him making it do so; show and help.

Inspector Wain was still smiling. He looked around the yard, came back to Ben and said, "Furthermore there's the matter of fingerprints."

"So?"

"Yours, Mr. Armitage, are on the rifle."

Ben blurted, "But that's impossible!"

"Not at all," Wain said, drawling the words as if he wanted to make them last. "I just got the report. Your fingerprints are definitely on the gun."

Ben felt himself getting dizzy. He put a hand on top of the car, the other to his brow. "My prints?"

"Exactly."

Ben raced his mind around—until he remembered. He squeezed his eyes closed. He saw himself and Jill. They were in her living room. Because he had put into her mind how beautiful it was, she was polishing the gun. She had cleaned it of prints. But then when he had taken it for her into the bedroom, he had unwrapped it to put in the nine shells.

Ben opened his eyes, dropped his hands. "Yes, I recall now. Hey, you had me scared for a minute there."

Inspector Wain's smile smoothed out. He said, "Naturally you have an explanation."

"Listen. It slipped my mind. A dear friend was dead in my arms. I wasn't fully aware of what I was doing, of putting Val down and running outside. This was when Harry was in the parlour, telephoning. You see?"

"Go on."

"I ran out full of rage and grief. I couldn't see anyone. I did notice the gun. I picked it up, looked at it, dropped it again, and went quickly back to Val. That's all."

Wain said a tired, "That's not quite up to your usual slick standard."

Ben had his confidence back. He had relegated the prints to a lower position. As always, Ben found it simple to suppress the irksome. He said,

"Oh look, Wain. Let's stop playing games. You haven't a thing. The bits you're trying to make stick together, they could be blasted in court by any competent lawyer."

"You think so?"

"Yes, and so do you. You're going to need a lot more proof."

The detective dropped his foot from the bumper. "We'll see," he said. He turned and moved away.

Ben bent down to get in the patrol car. He was sure that Wain was beginning to have serious doubts about his original theory, and he hadn't even heard yet of Jill's confession. All was well.

The sergeant got in at Ben's side. The constable started the car and steered it forward. They went out of the yard, along an alley and turned onto the front street.

Near the entrance to the police station stood the Hillman convertible. Jill was at the wheel. Leaning down talking to her was Inspector Wain. Lounging against the wall of the building were three reporters. They looked bored.

As the patrol car drove by, Wain opened the Hillman's passenger door and got in.

Ben didn't look back. He was thoughtful. Jill, he realised, could not have confessed to the police or to anyone who would make a police report. Yet confessed she had. It might have been to a close friend, or a child, or it might not have been to a human being at all. She could have talked to an animal, or to herself in a mirror.

Ben told himself that it was his own fault. He should have been more explicit in his orders. But the mistake was understandable, and could be easily rectified. Easily.

Ben folded his arms to counter a swoop of pleasure. He felt again, as so often before, that joy in pure power. He was the puppeteer, the manipulator, the man in charge. He could understand now why so many in history had preferred to remain an eminence grise rather than grab the top post. And in his own case, it was without connexions, strings, that he had been and still was in absolute control.

Ben thought it probable that Jill Parr had no unusual gifts whatever. All the strength and talent was his. Jill was merely a receiving set, like thousands and maybe millions of others. It was a case of a strong will dominating the weaker.

Domination. Ben liked that concept. He mused that a man with the lust to succeed, plus of course the mental strength, could rise to a position of awesome power. It might take a lifetime of dedication. But what an achievement. Working through the medium of, say, television, that man could become the mind of his generation, could tell the masses what to think, how to vote. All he need do to get himself into the right position for that, was control the mind of each man ahead of him on the ladder. The climb would be sure, the end result an orgy of joy.

Ben shivered. He tightened the clench of his folded arms and stared ahead with a dreamy smile.

"Power," Jill said.

Inspector Wain turned to look at her. "I beg you pardon, Miss Parr?"

She didn't answer. Only vaguely had she been aware of speaking and of being addressed, just as she was not giving herself fully to the task of controlling the car. She drove automatically.

Jill felt a curious elation. It didn't fit with her other feelings. It was like trying to smile with cracked lips. Jill's basic spirits were cowed.

The shock which had started with her assumption that she had killed, and that the one she had killed was Ben, had been progressing with the implacable stealth of a hidden disease. It had been further helped along by what Ben had said in the detention room, and by the terrifying urge to confess. After being arrested at that stage on answering the urge, progress had been vastly accelerated when she had gone out of her flat to set off for Cranwell.

First Jill had seen a dent in her car. It was new. As it was on the inner side, it could not have been made by a passing vehicle. But it did fit with something she remembered about a nightmare of a drive.

Next, having got inside the Hillman, Jill had found on the

floor a piece of canvas. It fitted with what she knew, or had dreamt, of a rifle.

Jill was suffering a concussion of the senses. She was close to entering a catatonic state. No longer did she recall having thrown the canvas out of the window as she drove, nor any other detail of the drive itself.

Only when nearing a forked junction with a telephone booth had Jill recollected that she should not be here, that she had to go to a police station. Once she had found it, she sat outside in the car until the detective had come.

There had been other thoughts in Jill's mind as well as that one about power; but they had been too fast for her to embrace, or too meaningless for her to examine.

Now the elation went. Jill slumped a little lower in the seat.

She steered around a bend in the lane. Ahead was a telephone box. Again she was approaching that junction. She reached it and bore to the right.

A voice spoke. When it spoke a second time, Jill roused herself with an effort and asked, "What?"

"'Do you know the way,' I said."

"Where?"

Turning toward her the detective said, "The Farnsworth place."

"No. I'm sorry. I can't help you."

"That's all right," he said, turning back slowly. "I know the way. In fact, here we are."

"Here we are," Jill echoed, dutiful. She began to slow her Hillman, drawing into the side near the overhanging oak.

"No," the detective said. "I meant there, the white gate."

Jill picked up speed again. She drove on, reached the gateway and steered through. A moment later she was easing to a stop behind a police car. Beyond that, in the centre of a patch of gravel, stood three men. Two were in uniform. The other was Ben. There was a house.

The house and the two cars and the gravel and the surrounding trees—they had a familiarity for Jill that caused her fear. A plaintive, minor, distant voice told her that this was one of those sensations of having been somewhere before. It made no difference. The fear lived. Jill retreated further into herself.

The driver's door was opened by the detective. Jill got out. "Excuse me," the man said. He walked away to join the others. Jill stayed where she was. She waited. She was waiting with a quiet dread to be told what to do or think next.

"About here," Ben said, waving his arm downward. "Roughly. It was dark, remember, and I was pretty frantic. But about here would be right."

Inspector Wain asked, "You simply picked it up and put it down again?"

"No, not snap-snap like that. I held it while I went on looking around. There was nothing to see or hear."

"No footsteps? Sounds of running? A crashing through the trees? A car leaving?"

"Not that I can recall, no," Ben said, frowning as if trying to remember the important. "In fact, no, obviously."

"Why obviously?"

"Well, if I'd heard anything I would instinctively have gone chasing after it, the way I'd come running out here."

Wain nodded. "So you put the gun down and went back in."

"Dropped it."

"You might be interested to know," the inspector said, "that yours are the only prints on the gun."

Ben lifted his arms. "That's not surprising. Killers usually have the sense to wear gloves. I would have myself, if I'd planned to do this."

"Possibly it was on the spur of the moment."

Ben smiled. "And I just happened to have a rifle along with me? Oh sure."

Inspector Wain's answer was to turn and walk away. He went back to the convertible, where he took Jill by the elbow. She glanced up at him and then allowed herself to be led forward. Her walk was stiff.

Looks like a zombie, Ben thought. Looks like something that should be put away, or put down. Looks like a vegetable. And that is the pathetic creature who has destroyed my happiness.

Ben felt a lump swell in his throat. He looked away and lifted a hand to his neck, which he stroked gently. The cavity throbbed in his chest.

But you can surmount this, Ben told himself. You can leave it behind. You're young and uniquely gifted. There is a lifetime of conquest ahead.

The sound of shoes on gravel brought Ben's eyes around again. After a presence of mere seconds, the lump in his throat was receding before the cure of ego, the sore-rimmed hole in his chest was back to its bearable depth.

Inspector Wain and Jill were nearing the cottage door. Jill seemed to be interested in the far distance. She failed to do the expected—glance over at Ben.

He thought: Zombie.

Jill's lips moved.

Wain produced the house keys and unlocked the door. Standing it wide open, he led Jill inside and took her from view into the living room.

The sergeant touched Ben's arm as he moved forward. Ben kept pace. The constable followed. The trio walked at a solemn, measured tread that made Ben think fleetingly of thirteen steps.

At the house he moved ahead and went in first. The hall had a lingering smell of burned sauce. Ben kept his mind on that, and off the place underfoot where Val had lain, as he passed through into the parlour.

Jill was sitting on the couch, on the edge of the cushions. Her spine she held straight. Her face was directed toward the empty fireplace. Her hands were clasped loosely in the sailors' grip. At the movement of entry she didn't look around.

Inspector Wain stood at one side of the hearth, his feet spread, his back to the mantelpiece. He was striking a match to put to the cigarette in his oversize lips.

Instead of going right into the room, Ben came to a stop just beyond the threshold. It had occurred to him, for the first time, that last night he himself, unsuspecting, even amused at the coincidence of a knock sounding in time with his thoughts, could have gone to the door and opened it and been shot. He shuddered.

"Feeling all right, Mr. Armitage?"

The speaker was Inspector Wain. He had his eyes on Ben in a casual-seeming but watchful way, like a cat's on a distant dog.

Ben tongued the backs of his teeth to bring moisture into his mouth. He looked at Jill, the picture of peace, and his unsteadiness turned to anger. With equal speed, he saw the way to immediate release and revenge.

The detective repeated, "Feeling all right, Mr. Armitage?"

Ben said, "No."

He would do it now, that was the answer. He would make her confess here, in the right place, at the right time—under the watch of her puppeteer. She wouldn't be able to make any clever evasions.

Wain asked, "What is it?"

Ben gestured around the room. "It's the cottage. Val. Death. The whole thing."

"Yes, I see."

"I'm upset," Ben said. "It hasn't been easy, holding all of this in. Val was a wonderful person."

Inspector Wain nodded. He looked away, turned his eyes down to Jill. Ben asked, "Would you mind if I stepped outside for a minute or two? Have a little think. You know."

Wain answered without turning his head. "Very well."

"Alone, if you don't mind."

"I don't, Mr. Armitage."

"I won't run away."

"I'm sure you won't," Inspector Wain said. "All right, a couple of minutes."

Ben turned and walked out.

When Ben's footfalls had faded, the parlour was silent. It might have been deserted rather than owning the presence of four people.

The sergeant had sat down on a straight chair at the back of the room. He was an older man, stout, fluffy grey hair showing under the rim of his helmet. His pale blue eyes were fixed wistfully on the cigarette his superior was smoking.

The constable stood by the door. Young, his face had the freshness of new-chopped wood. He told of his enthusiasm for his job by being stiffly in the stand-easy position, hands held behind. But he rocked gently back and forth on his toes.

Inspector Wain was still by the hearth. He now leaned on the mantel and rested an arm along the wood. His pose had become more jaunty. He crossed his legs at the ankles.

It was as if the detective were hoping to hide the keenness in his face by drawing attention to the light-hearted stance. He looked at Jill with an expression that seemed to combine interest and concern.

Jill stared into the dead, grey hearth.

Jill had returned to her emptiness. Arrival indoors had been strange. While sitting, there had come a rapid jumble of thought, along with feelings of sadness and rage and satisfaction, the whole rushing so much as if in panic that her head had swirled. Calm had settled.

Jill was waiting.

Now, her wait ended. A twitching ripple moved across her face as the command came. It was not the same as before. But it was hers. She was talking to herself inside. She accepted it and spoke it aloud.

Jill's words, unexpected, rang oddly in the silent room. She said, "Speak, you fool."

The sergeant sat up straighter. The constable stopped rocking on his toes. Inspector Wain, frowning to give himself a more acute stare, uncrossed his legs with a slowness and care that suggested he was afraid of being noticed.

"Speak," Jill said. "Speak."

There were only the slightest of lip movements accompanying the words. Her face was slack, lifeless. It matched the tone of her voice.

Jill spoke without emotion, without change of pitch, without measurement. It was a droning sound. It was like a priest's chant reduced to a whisper.

"Get it out," she said.

Inspector Wain licked his lips. He glanced quickly at the other two officers, brought down his arm from the mantelshelf, eased away from the lean.

Jill said, "Speak up."

Wain noticed the smoke curling up in front of his face. Frowning at that feeble block to his view of the woman on the couch, he tossed his cigarette behind him into the fireplace.

Using a low voice, like that of someone worried about waking a sleeper, Inspector Wain asked, "What was that, Miss Parr?"

Jill ignored the question. She hadn't heard it. Feeling more weirdly empty than ever, she was concentrating on reading off the words that came forcefully into her mind, the words she was speaking to herself.

"Get it all out," she said in her dull, quiet monotone. "Let's hear it."

Ben was near a corner of the cottage. Since coming outside he had been standing in this same place, and in the same pose: his back in a crouch, his head down, his eyes tightly closed, his fingers pressed to the sides of his brow and describing small circles.

Slowly, carefully, with all the force and passion he owned, Ben had been working at mind control. At no time during the weeks of his telepathic aims had he strove with such strength and determination.

Here, at this perfect psychological time and place, Jill had to confess in order to make him free and to bring on herself everything she deserved.

Ben pictured Jill sitting on the couch, but zoomed in to fill his mind with her face when forcing the words away from himself. He sweated. Water oozed from him due to effort; and from the suspense.

Was he having success? Was she reacting well?

Ben's desire to know, it began interfering with his concentration. The picture flickered, his words left weakly. He would have to settle the question.

Straightening, Ben stepped to the corner of the house. With his back to the wall he sidled along until he came within a foot of the parlour window. He stopped.

There was no sound to be heard from inside. But then came a question from Inspector Wain. The detective asked gently, "Could you repeat that, please, Miss Parr?"

Ben closed his eyes, fingered his temples and thought: Got to tell. Got . . .

He broke off as, from inside, he heard Jill saying a split second behind his thoughts, "Got to tell. Got . . ."

Jubilant, Ben moved back from the window. Swiftly and softly he returned to the corner. There, his excitement and elation rose to an irresistible pitch.

He doubled up with silent laughter.

In the parlour, the three policemen started nervously when, without warning, Jill Parr began to laugh.

Her head drooped. She let her trunk sag forward. She had no expression apart from the open mouth. Her arms flopped down like dangled ropes so that her hands nuzzled the carpet.

Jill felt amused without knowing why. Head and shoulders trembling, she produced a curious laughter sound, dry, rhythmic. It was similar to a gentle handclap.

The sergeant rose in aching slowness from his chair. His face gave the impression that he was watching something lewd. The young constable looked sickened.

Inspector Wain was standing tautly erect. For a moment it appeared as though he would move forward, either to speak to Jill or to touch her. Then he did neither.

Jill came to the end of her chain of laughter sounds. She sighed. Except for reclasping her hands on her lap, she did not return to her former position. She stayed in a forward sag, her blank face aimed toward the hearthrug.

She sighed again and spoke. In that same dead voice she said, "All right. Clearly. Like this." Following a pause, she added, "I want to tell you everything."

Inspector Wain moved one quiet step closer.

"I want to tell you about Val," Jill said. "I hated her. She was going to take Ben away from me. She loved him desperately. She loved him more than anything else in the world. She was prepared to go to any lengths to get Ben for herself. He didn't realise that. He thought they were just friends. But she was determined to have him and she would have won in the end."

Jill stared on at the hearthrug. She said, "Val had to die. I love Ben too. I had to stop Val before it was too late. She was so beautiful, she couldn't lose."

Inspector Wain drew in a long, deep, shaky breath. He let it out again while smiling.

Jill went on in a drone, "It's being back here that makes me want to tell the truth. It was a mistake to come. You would never have found out. No proof. I stole the gun and ammunition. I'll tell you about that later. I wore gloves when I drove out here last night. No one saw me. I came through the trees. I knocked on the door and moved back. When she came out, I shot her. I dropped the gun and ran."

After a pause, Jill said, "That's all there is. I killed Valerie Farnsworth. I am sorry."

Inspector Wain had stopped smiling. His face was sad. It was as if he had lost something. He moved forward and stopped at Jill's side. Bending, he said quietly,

"Shall we go, Miss Parr?"

There was no response. Wain made to reach for Jill's arm, but stopped when she spoke again. She said, with no change in tone or expression:

"Now. Is that all? Have I left anything out? Or rather, is there anything I can put in to make me cleaner?"

Wain blinked. He straightened up.

"Ammo," Jill said. "The box. Could I put it in Jill's flat? No, too risky. I'll get rid of it as soon as I'm home, when they've stuck dear Jill in a cell and let me go. What else?"

Inspector Wain, eyes bright and stance taut, glanced once toward the window before returning his stare to Jill.

She said, "That girl at the Leicester Square range. She fancied me. But she wouldn't remember. I was just one man among a hundred a day. And that was weeks ago. But shooting. Out by the old football club. That young couple saw me. So what? They'll never turn up. Probably from miles away, won't even remember, just there for a fast roll in the hay. No, that's fine. Everything's fine. Madam Zena you can forget. I'm golden. It's tight and right."

Jill finished speaking. Silence returned to the parlour.

There was no hint of emotion in Jill's face or position. The two uniformed men were tensely alert, both watching their superior the way soldiers watch for news of an order before it's spoken.

Inspector Wain continued to stare down at Jill for a moment. Then he stepped back to the hearth and took up his former lean on the mantelpiece.

Half a minute passed. The silence went on. The four people stayed exactly as they were.

There came the sound of footsteps on gravel. A shadow moved across the window. More footsteps, now on floorboards, and Ben walked into the parlour.

Ben was close to trembling with pleasure and confidence, and with excitement over a future that looked so grand. He felt poignant out of love for himself.

By working at cleverly veiling the look of triumph he sent to Jill, Ben failed to notice that he was being watched carefully by the three policemen.

He said, "I'm a lot better now. Sorry about that. We can get on with it."

Wain asked blandly, "On with what?"

"Your re-enactment."

"Oh, I don't think there's any need for that, Armitage."

Ben, uncomprehending but not disturbed, "Oh?"

"I'm fairly sure it was done just as I theorised," Inspector Wain said. "And I doubt if you would repeat that performance for us."

Ben glanced at Jill, at the sergeant, and behind at the young constable. Jill hadn't changed, but he noted now the difference in the men. He asked an unsteady, "What is this?"

Inspector Wain stood erect from the mantel. He said, "Where exactly in your flat is the box of two-two ammunition?"

Outwardly calm but thinking busily, Ben said, "I don't know what you mean." At which same moment, her words under his, Jill said in a bleak chant,

"This has to be a bluff."

Ben blinked as his cheeks twitched. His heart began to tap above normal. He struggled for recovery.

Wain said a conversational, "The couple near the old football club, the girl in Leicester Square, Madam Zena. Care to tell us about those people?"

Ben stared. He couldn't believe what he had heard. Nor what he heard next, from Jill. She said,

"No. The bastard's bluffing, guessing. He couldn't know a thing about . . ."

The words trailed off as Ben turned his stare on Jill. His mouth sagged. Jill monotoned, "What's she saying? Christ, what's she saying?"

Ben gaped in horror.

Inspector Wain came forward from the hearth. He stood in front of Ben. In a hard voice he said, "Benjamin Armitage, I have here a warrant for your arrest."

While Ben went on staring, Jill said, "No no no."

Inspector Wain, "You are charged with the murder of one Valerie Farnsworth."

Jill said, "Insane. Mad. I don't believe it."

Wain, "It is my duty to warn you that anything you say will be taken down in writing and may be used against you in evidence."

Jill said, "Jesus Christ."

I 21   Staring, his face stupidly slack, Ben began to back away.

Jill said in her dead voice, "This isn't happening. It's mad. I don't believe it. This can't happen to me."

Suddenly, Ben whirled and ran out of the room.

The young constable quickly followed. After a brief hesitation, surprised, the sergeant did the same. The sound of rapid footfalls on gravel could be heard. The sound faded.

Inspector Wain sighed. His body sagged. He put his hands behind, lowered his head, and walked out slowly after the others.

The parlour was silent again. Jill sat as before, features and eyes without expression. After a moment she began to speak. She chanted tonelessly, "Mummy, Mummy, help me, Mummy."